Don't miss an exciting new book by

international bestselling author

Barbara McMahon

in

Harlequin Romance®

*Barbara McMahon creates stories bubbling
with warmth and emotion. Her captivating
style and believable characters will leave
your romance senses tingling!*

**If you fall in love with Sheikh Talique...
then don't miss Barbara's next prince of the
desert in an exciting new Harlequin Romance
continuity: THE BRIDES OF BELLA LUCIA, where
Sheikh Surim will sweep you off your feet.**

The Sheikh and the Nanny—January 2007
#3928

"Lunch in the air?" Laura asked.

"I thought it might be enjoyable. Or we can wait until we land."

"I don't believe I've ever had such an extravagant date. This is so much fun!"

Talique nodded. It didn't hurt to enjoy himself while moving his plan forward. For minutes at a time he could forget the reason he was here and enjoy Laura's company. She was not as accomplished as his ex-wife had been, lacking a certain amount of sophistication with her wide-eyed appreciation of everything. It was refreshing in a way, but he couldn't let himself think that way. He had to remember the past.

"Are you happy, Laura?"

Laura was having the best time of her life. Everything was perfect....

THE SHEIKH'S
SECRET

Barbara McMahon

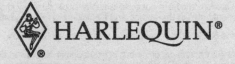

HARLEQUIN®

TORONTO • NEW YORK • LONDON
AMSTERDAM • PARIS • SYDNEY • HAMBURG
STOCKHOLM • ATHENS • TOKYO • MILAN • MADRID
PRAGUE • WARSAW • BUDAPEST • AUCKLAND

ISBN-13: 978-0-373-03899-2
ISBN-10:   0-373-03899-2

THE SHEIKH'S SECRET

First North American Publication 2006.

www.eHarlequin.com

Printed in U.S.A.

Barbara McMahon was born and raised in the South, but settled in California after spending a year flying around the world for an international airline. After settling down to raise a family and work for a computer firm, she began writing when her children started school. Now, feeling fortunate in being able to realize a long-held dream of quitting her "day job" and writing full-time, she and her husband have moved to the Sierra Nevada of California, where she finds her desire to write is stronger than ever. With the beauty of the mountains visible from her windows, and the pace of life slower than the hectic San Francisco Bay area where they previously resided, she finds more time than ever to think up stories and characters and share them with others through writing.

Barbara loves to hear from readers. You can reach her at P.O. Box 977, Pioneer, CA 95666-0977, U.S.A. Readers can also contact Barbara at her Web site: www.barbaramcmahon.com

CHAPTER ONE

San Francisco, California

LAURA TOLIVER stepped off the elevator to the floor that housed Beatty Security. It was Saturday, not a day she normally worked, but after last night's showing, she wanted to write her report while it was fresh and not have to wait until Monday. She had nothing else planned for the weekend. It would take an hour or so and then she'd be free.

There were others working and she waved to a couple of them as she passed. They were hunched over their computers, or talked on the phone. Beatty Securities ran a full service bureau, with operatives and personnel on duty 24/7.

Her boss was in his office. He looked up as she passed the opened door.

"Laura?" he called.

She backed up and peeked in. "Yes?"

He stood and tossed a newspaper to the far edge of his desk. "Have you seen this?"

She entered the cluttered office and picked up the

LifeStyle section of the *San Francisco News*. Her face smiled back at her. Beside her stood Sheikh Yuusuf ibn Horah in all his gorgeous good looks.

"I remember when they snapped it. I had just finished the first circle of the museum and had joined Jenna and Yuusuf for a few minutes." Laura placed the newspaper back on the desk. "A problem?"

"Only if it gets out that you work for our security firm. We want unobtrusive surveillance at these events, not have every thief around know what our operatives look like," Ben said.

"There's no problem, boss. As far as anyone knows, except Jenna and Yuusuf, I was a guest there like everyone else."

"Hmm." He seemed mollified and sat back down in his chair. "What're you doing here today? After such a late shift last night, I'd think you'd sleep in. Especially since it's Saturday."

"I wanted to get the report filed. I have some photos of people I wanted to do a trace on. Nothing specific, just vague feelings."

Laura had worked for Beatty Security for three years. Her speciality was guarding museum pieces on display. She was available, as most operatives were, for other functions as they arose. She did not carry a gun, but had been trained in martial arts. Her primary function was to mingle, keep an eye on the priceless artifacts and identify anyone who showed an undue interest in the items Beatty Security was hired to guard. She had several discreet miniature cameras and easily took photos of anyone who merited a closer look.

"I trust your judgment," he said. "But don't spend all your free weekend in the office."

She smiled and turned to head for her desk. "No worries there. It's too glorious today to stay inside if I don't have to. I won't be long and then I'm off to Golden Gate Park for some biking."

When Laura reached her desk, she fished the small digital camera from her purse and uploaded the photos onto her computer. She had obtained the names of the people she photographed and quickly ran them through some of the standard databases available to compile a brief dossier on anyone a Beatty Security person thought needed watching.

Oh, oh, she thought a few minutes later. Warren Way, the older man she'd almost convinced herself was just very enthusiastic, had a rap sheet. Wasn't that interesting? She printed his photo and the background results to circulate among the others in the company. He'd be identified for future functions and watched.

Her phone rang.

"Toliver," she responded, beginning to type her report.

"Hey, Laura, go find your own guy," Jenna Stanhope said, laughter in her tone.

"I should be so lucky to find one like Yuusuf. How did the photographer get my face and not yours? I could swear you were draped over Yuusuf all night like a sarape," Laura responded.

"Hah! We may be growing close, but are circumspect. That's why the speculation in the article that accompanied the photo. Who is the eligible bachelor after now? What a hoot."

"There was more?" Laura asked. She'd only glanced at the picture. "What did it say?"

"Just gossipy speculation on the sheikh's latest interest."

"My boss is worried my cover will be blown."

"Not with this article. It's more like everyone in San Francisco will think you and Yuusuf are having a red-hot affair. I ought to be jealous."

Laura laughed. "As if he'd even look at me when you're around. He has eyes for you alone and you know it."

"You never can tell," Jenna said.

"Look, I know I warned you against him when you first started seeing him. He does have a reputation as a playboy, you know," Laura said. "Before you, rumor has it, he never dated a woman more than three times before dumping her."

"Lies all of them. That's what everyone says about sheikhs, it goes with the territory. Although, he's had a couple of bad experiences with women, but it wasn't his fault."

"Like what?"

"They wanted his money."

"Maybe. Just be careful, okay? I know he looks too be too good to be true, and I'm always leery about men like that," Laura said.

"You're leery about all men."

"Am not. Just cautious. Anyway, since I've come to know him better, he seems to be a good guy."

"Stop being cautious and be more like me and you'll find your own good guy. If Mr. Right comes along, you won't recognize him if you don't give yourself a chance, and then where will you be?"

"I'm not sure there is a Mr. Right as you say. I'd settle for a Mr. This-is-as-good-as-it-gets," Laura said wryly.

"You only say that because you haven't met the love of your life yet. I think you're too picky."

"So does this mean you've met the love of your life, or that you aren't so picky?"

"I think I have," Jenna said quietly.

"Yuusuf?" Laura sat up at that. Was her friend serious?

"He's really all I could ever want," Jenna said.

"You two haven't known each other long enough to know that," Laura argued.

"Haven't you heard of love at first sight?"

"Have you heard of marry in haste, repent at leisure?"

Jenna was quiet for a moment. She'd been married at twenty-one and divorced eighteen months later.

"Oh, jeez, I'm sorry, Jens. I didn't mean Phil. I meant don't you rush into anything. If it's the real deal, it'll last forever, so why rush?" Laura sometimes forgot about Phil. He'd been gone for six years. Still, it had been a bad time for her friend and the last thing she wanted was to remind her.

"I still believe in love at first sight," Jenna said stubbornly.

"I might, if I ever found it." Laura had never been in love before. She dated, of course and had had a steady relationship with a man when they were both in college. Just prior to graduation, they broke it off and she hardly suffered a pang, much less anything like the ache of heartbreak.

She was twenty-eight now. Maybe she was destined to be like her friend's Aunt Kendra, single at fifty. She yearned to believe in love at first sight, to dream about meeting some man who would sweep her off her feet and carry her away. Have him date her with all the love in the world and wind up with a happy marriage and two or three children.

Each time she met a new man, she wondered if something would click. Each time, she found they were entertaining or funny or intense. But there was never that spark that would light her fire.

"Yuusuf is taking me sailing today on the Bay. Want to join us?" Jenna asked.

"And be a fifth wheel? I don't think so. You two have fun. Just take things more slowly, okay?"

"I don't think he's after my money. He has as much wealth as I do."

"I find that hard to believe." Jenna was from an old San Francisco family who started building the family fortune at the time of the Gold Rush. Each generation had added to the coffers, including her software engineer father. As an only child, Jenna was the sole heiress to the fortune when her parents died.

She'd made friends with Laura when they'd both been little girls, long before anyone in Laura's family knew of the Stanhopes's wealth. Their friendship had grown and survived high school and college. It continued strong and lasting despite their different lifestyles and circumstances.

"You do like him, right?" Jenna asked.

"Of course I do. He's charming and fun to be around.

I enjoyed talking to him last night while you were visiting with other friends. I don't have anything bad to say about him, just be careful. I'd hate for you to fall for him and then find he's only having fun while he works in San Francisco. Won't he be returning home at some point?"

"I don't know. Maybe he can continue to run their family office here and we can settle in the city."

"Have your parents met him yet?" Laura asked.

"No. I want him all to myself for a little longer. But I'll introduce him soon. I don't want speculation if I'm reading things wrong. Or Dad's cross-examination ruined what we have."

Laura laughed. "Your dad's just doing what dads do." For a moment Laura wished she had a father living to act that way. Even her beloved grandfather was gone. "I've got to get to work. Want to have dinner one night next week?" she asked, shaking off the sadness.

"When?"

"I have a commitment on Tuesday and on Friday, so any other night is fine."

"Wednesday, then. I'll leave Friday open in case Yuusuf wants to do something," Jenna said.

"Have fun, just take it slow," Laura said before she hung up. She was happy for Jenna—as long as Yuusuf didn't break her heart. If he did, he'd answer to her!

Turning back to the report, she forgot about the picture in the paper. Her cover had not been blown, the gossip in the accompanying article had strengthened the idea she was a guest at the showing. That was what mattered most.

Tamarin

Talique bin Azoz bin Al-Rahman entered the house of his grandfather. He'd been summoned and hoped it was somehow business related and had nothing to do with his grandfather's frail health. He had a deadline looming for negotiations with the dock managers in Germany to make sure the cruise ships were given priority treatment when they brought tourists to the country. Yet he never was too consumed by work to ignore a family matter.

His grandfather rarely requested his presence on such short notice. There had to be something wrong. Tal just hoped it was a minor inconvenience in the greater scheme of things. His mother had not mentioned anything when he'd last spoken to her. Surely she'd know if something was wrong with her father.

He was announced and Sheikh Ali Salilk ibn Horah rose from the sofa where he sat and turned to greet his oldest grandson. More frail than Tal had ever remembered, he still had that fire in his eyes, and military-straight posture that Tal always associated with him.

"Ah, Talique, thank you for coming. I know you are a busy man, but I require your assistance."

"Grandfather," Tal said, bowing his head slightly in formal acknowledgment. "How may I help?"

Salilk picked up a foreign newspaper and held it out to Tal. He took it, scanning it briefly, stopping when he saw the picture of his cousin Yuusuf. A twinge of apprehension hit. Yuusuf was still in the United States—San Francisco to be exact. He was working with the expansion of the import-export concern the family held.

The photo was clear. It had been taken at some museum showing. The woman photographed with him was tall and slender with short, dark hair, and wide eyes. She didn't look his cousin's usual type which ran to blond and built.

Tal stifled a sigh of resignation. It looked as if Yuusuf was not adhering to the agreement they'd set down after the last fortune hunter almost caught him in her trap. Why was he so easily enamored with foreign women?

"Read the article," his grandfather said, sitting back against the luscious cushions on the low settee. "A member of our embassy in Los Angeles sent it. I'm most distressed. After that last fiasco with the woman in Los Angeles, I thought he'd settled down. Now it looks as if he's getting involved with this woman. This has to stop, Tal. I cannot afford to let my grandson get tangled up with mercenary women wherever he goes."

Tal knew firsthand about the situations his cousin fell into. Hadn't he been instrumental in rescuing him time and again?

Tal quickly scanned the article, the innuendoes familiar. His cousin was known as a ladies' man, eagerly dating all the beautiful women who flocked around him. Twice he had come close to succumbing to the deliberate lures of outright money grabbers. It looked as if he was heading that way yet a third time. Tal wanted to throw the paper across the room and storm out. He didn't have time for this. He had exacted a promise from his cousin after the last time he'd rescued him. What was Yuusuf doing now?

"I don't know what's wrong with the boy," Salilk said, rising again as if unable to sit still. He paced to the wide window. "He knows he has a duty to his family. And it does not include dallying with women wherever he goes. Why can't he be more like you? You followed tradition. You went to school in England as your father and I did—not America. You married the woman your father picked out, rather than get embroiled in a scandal with someone who only wanted your money. You have taken the reins of one of your father's businesses, rather than roaming the world and spending more time away from home than here."

Tal listened impassively as his grandfather let off steam comparing his life with that of his cousin's. Inside he wasn't the golden-child the family thought. True he'd followed the education tradition but only because it suited him to attend school in England. He had British friends with whom he kept in touch and often visited London when he wanted a break. Friends and acquaintances who proved to be invaluable contacts for business were one result of following family tradition.

His marriage to Yasmine had been arranged by their parents. Initially it had suited him. She'd been an accomplished hostess, spoken three languages and been a true asset for a businessman on the rise.

He had hoped he and his bride would come to hold each other in great affection, as his parents did. Bleakly he had to acknowledge it had never come close. Yasmine had coveted his wealth to open doors, to enable her to travel, buy designer gowns and costly jewels.

Her death had been unexpected and tragic. His family thought he grieved for her. In truth he was not sorry he was no longer married. He had never said a word against her, or revealed the loneliness he'd experienced in his own home. He would never wish such a relationship on his cousin. Yet why wouldn't Yuusuf learn to separate fortune hunters from a genuinely suitable prospect.

As to taking the reins of his father's shipping business, maybe Salilk should show as much wisdom as his own father had and relinquish some of his responsibilities so Yuusuf had a real place in the company, rather than *dallying* in San Francisco. His son, Yuusuf's father, had died young. Yuusuf's mother, French born Yvette, had remained in Tamirim. Her sister also lived in Tamarin and they had raised his cousin—with his grandfather's help and that of his own parents. Maybe Yvette should have had a stronger hand when raising Yuusuf. If his father had lived, things would have been different.

But Tal said none of this. He merely counted the moments until his grandfather finished his tirade and he could find out what specifically he wanted. Tal had a conference call in half hour, and needed to decide whether he was required in Bremerhaven or not.

"So once again I need your help in getting him untangled," Salilk finished, wheezing slightly. His health had been declining for a number of years, and Tal wanted nothing to hasten his decline.

Tal stared at him. Had he missed an important aspect of this conversation?

"You want *me* to get him out of this? I don't need to get involved. Tell him he has to come home. Or send the woman a large check and a warning. It'll get her to let go. Especially if you tell her as you did that one in Boston that you'll cut him off without a penny if he marries her." Yuusuf had been furious with Tal for his interference. Tal regretted the rift in their once-close tie.

"That's just it, my boy, weren't you listening? I don't want Yuusuf to know I'm objecting. After last time, he'll be that much more determined to prove to you and me that this woman wants him for himself. He knows I would never cut him off—not permanently. He's my oldest son's only child. I need you to go and get him out of this without him knowing we are behind it."

"We?"

Why was he the one chosen to rescue his cousin every time? Yvette was his mother, why not enlist her help? Tal knew—his grandfather would never ask for a woman's help. But family duty nagged at him.

"And how do you propose I handle this?" Tal asked, his annoyance growing.

"I have no idea. I leave that up to you. You have innovative ideas. You've increased profits at the cruise company more than twenty percent, so your father tells me. He and your mother are proud of you, my boy."

"I have to keep on top of things to keep that profit level high. I don't have time to go extricate Yuusuf from the clutches of some fortune hunter. Send someone else this time," Tal said in frustration. He was not a babysitter. Time his cousin grew up.

"Who else would he listen to?" Salilk asked. "He has admired you all his life. You are the older brother he doesn't have. You have to handle this. I cannot."

"He isn't going to listen to me! If he truly thinks he's in love, he'll be up in arms against anyone trying to change his mind. You know how stubborn he can be." Tal was tired of chasing after him. Yuusuf was only two years younger. If it were up to Tal, he'd let the man sink or swim. Maybe he'd learn something along the way.

Though Tal would draw the line at letting Yuusuf get married to some gold digger. Dammit, why couldn't Yuusuf keep his mind on business like Talique had learned to do?

"Find a way. I need you to save your cousin," his grandfather said firmly. "There is no one else I can trust to make sure he is not taken advantage of. Come, I do not ask much of you. You can help our family this way."

Tal fumed silently. It was the ultimate weapon and his grandfather knew it. His father often said how much he owed his wife's father for helping him through a bad patch in business many years ago. Their branch of the family would forever be in Salilk's debt. Tal assumed that obligation when he attained adulthood. Why had he thought logical business practice would take precedence? His position as head of the cruise ship line that plied the Mediterranean and Atlantic with small luxury liners was not an easy task. Competition was high, especially from the Greeks and Italians. But family came first. There was honor of their family debt at stake. And his grandfather's frail health.

Gazing out the window at the lush gardens his grandmother loved so much, Tal tried to calculate how much time he could devote to this situation. If his trip to Bremerhaven was not necessary, maybe he could take a few

days to go to San Francisco. Quickly he considered and
discarded ideas. What was the most expeditious way to
extricate Yuusuf and get him to understand once and for
all that this must not happen again. Tal had learned
from the bitter experience what a loveless marriage
could do to a man and he'd decided he'd save his cousin
from the same fate—just once more and this time it
would be final.

"Perhaps there is a way," Talique said slowly.
Looking at his uncle, he shrugged. "If we can turn the
woman away from Yuusuf, get her to show her true
colors, he'll be free of her machinations. And if I do it
right, maybe he'll learn a lesson about mercenary
women as well."

"Can you do that? What if she doesn't turn away?
Maybe I should insist he come home. He could get
angry, however, and do something rash. I regret again
that his father died so young. Yvette should have
married again."

"Maybe it's time he had someone turn him down. If
I can convince—" he looked at the paper again
"—Laura Toliver that I'm a better catch, without letting
Yuusuf know I'm around, she'll latch on to me. When
I leave, it'll be too bad for her, but Yuusuf will see her
for what she is."

"Chancy. What if Yuusuf finds out you are there? Or
she tells him about you?"

"I'll make sure I avoid Yuusuf. If he discovers I'm
there, it'll still give me a chance to show Laura I'm a
better choice. When she shifts her allegiance, I'll let all
parties know, and Yuusuf will see her for what she is.

Maybe it'll be a lesson learned that will stay with him a while. The last fiasco was only two years ago. The family can't go through that again."

Salilk beamed at Tal. "I knew I could count on you. He needs to come home, marry a woman his mother and I approve of and settle down. I would dearly love great-grandchildren."

Tal thought that was a bit much. His two sisters had provided his grandfather with five great-grandchildren between them.

"This is the last time. I got him out of the pickle with that girl in Boston. And the embarrassing scene with the woman in Los Angeles. I won't do it another time," Tal said, knowing it was a bluff. He would do whatever his grandfather asked. He would do anything to protect his family.

"I understand. He'll be more likely to listen to his mother's suggestions for a suitable wife if this woman turns away hoping to land a bigger fish. A brilliant plan," Salilk said beaming at his grandson. "Call me as soon as you've accomplished it."

CHAPTER TWO

San Francisco

LAURA WATCHED from the edge of the crowded ballroom. She and Jason were working tonight, watching for potential problems at the McNab's fundraiser. Patrick McNab, candidate for state senator, was schmoozing with the elite of San Francisco. Laura was sure she'd never seen so many rainbows shining from all the diamonds worn. Even the opera and other gala events she's worked hadn't brought out the gems like tonight's gathering. Everyone showing off, to hint where the true riches could be found, to woo a future senator.

All the more reason to be extra vigilant. She sipped her ginger ale, designed to look as if she were joining in with the champagne being poured as liberally as water. No alcohol for her or Jason. They had to stay alert.

She snapped a photo of Kyle Davenport. She knew about him and the rumors circulating about a downward change in fortunes for the flamboyant entrepreneur. Not that she expected any trouble from him, but it didn't hurt to update company files from time to time.

She let her gaze idly scan the room. Her eyes locked with the dark gaze of a stranger. He stood directly opposite her at the far wall. The bank of windows behind him gave way to a view of San Francisco at night that was breathtaking. But Laura didn't see the sparkling lights. For a moment, she saw only the tall man with the dark hair and compelling eyes. The rest of the lavishly appointed room and its occupants seemed to fade into a mist, leaving only the two of them.

Breaking eye contact took a major effort. She drew a deep breath forcing her gaze to move on. It was almost more of an effort than she could make to refrain from looking back. At least not yet. Maybe in a minute—

"Nice gathering," a deep voice said from her right. "Think he'll win the election?"

She knew who it was without turning. Drawing on a strength she hadn't known she had to calm suddenly riotous nerves, she slowly turned until she faced him. He was several inches taller than she. Usually she met most men at eye level. His height made her feel at a disadvantage.

"If he's the most qualified candidate," she said.

"I thought American politics was more about the man with the most charisma or the most money. I didn't realize other qualifications played into it."

He had a British accent, but his olive skin, dark eyes and jet-black hair hinted at other origins. Had she heard traces of a more exotic cadence in his tone?

"Sometimes it may appear that way, but usually the American public is savvy enough to vote for the best qualified man. Not always, however." Laura didn't want to discuss politics. She wanted to find out more about the man. Could his eyes really be so dark? His black hair gleamed beneath the chandeliers, with a slight wave that softened his austere looks. Who was he? And why was he talking to her?

"And this man's chances?" he asked, holding her gaze, as if he found the conversation fascinating. Or maybe it was her he found fascinating. Wishful thinking on her part.

"I think Patrick McNab has as good a chance as anyone," Laura said, not knowing or caring a bit about McNab's politics. She was here on assignment. Still, to keep it low profile, she needed to maintain at least the semblance of being a supporter if not a friend. She found it hard to remember why she was present when the stranger's eyes held hers. Her heart beat heavily, her skin warmed. She felt shy and breathless and bold and daring.

"I'm Tal," the man said, holding out his hand.

"I'm Laura," she replied, slipping hers into his. His was warm, his grip firm, but it did not linger beyond what was appropriate for a first greeting. Still, the contact left her feeling confused.

"I don't think you're from San Francisco," she said slowly, smiling. She hoped to draw him out. She loved English accents. And she was curious about the man. A quick glance at his left hand show it was ringless. But did that necessarily mean anything?

"Perceptive. Is it the accent? I flew in earlier today from London."

"It's a bit obvious, but charming. No jet lag?"

"I'm running on adrenaline. But I can adjust to California time sooner if I stay up until a reasonable time tonight. Then sleep through until morning. Tomorrow I'll be fine."

"Sounds like you've done that before," she said, wondering how often he came to San Francisco and how long he was staying this trip.

"Works every time."

"Staying long?" Laura asked. What do you do? Where are you staying? Do you have any free time to spend with me?

"For a few days. I take it you're a native?"

"Born and bred in the city. I'd be glad to show you around if you haven't seen it before," she said. Then was horrified. She never offered to act as tour guide, especially to someone she'd met less than five minutes before. Yet she couldn't let this one moment in time be all they had.

There was something about Tal that drew her like nothing before. Was he a con artist she should be wary of, or merely a stranger visiting San Francisco from England? Who did he know who would bring him to such an event?

"If you aren't supporting Mr. McNab, how did you get in?" she asked suddenly suspicious. She was too good at her job to get distracted for long.

"Earl Rogers is a big McNab supporter. His plans were made when I arrived unexpectedly, so he included me tonight. I've met the future senator. Can't say I'm ready to throw money into an election coffer for a man I hardly know, but maybe my host will convince me he's worth supporting."

"An Englishman supporting an American election?"

"Sometimes a good cause is worth supporting no matter where it is."

"So you're here on business, then?" Laura hoped she didn't sound like an inquisitor, but she wanted to find out all she could about the man. Did he withhold his last name deliberately, knowing how intriguing it was to be on first name terms yet not have a clue about each other's surnames? Or was there a reason to hide it?

"Part business, part pleasure." He looked around. "Are you here with someone?"

"No." Her heart rate sped up. Maybe he'd take her up on her offer to show him around.

He looked at her, his eyes dark and penetrating. Laura felt he saw right down into the heart of her. For a moment there was a gleam of hardness that startled her, then his friendly demeanor resurfaced. Had she imagined it? A trick of lighting?

"I'm surprised," he said. "A woman as lovely as you should be surrounded by men."

She didn't know whether to be insulted or flattered. Did he say what he thought women wanted to hear? What did that say about the kind he hung out with? She was not gorgeous, but looked nice enough. Not the type of woman who would have men flocking around, nor know what to do with them if they did.

Yet maybe he was trying to flatter her by implying

he thought she looked nice. Before she could decide which way to take the comment, her colleague Jason walked over, his eye on Tal.

"Jason. I'd like you to meet Tal." She smiled apologetically at Tal. "I'm sorry, I didn't get your last name."

"Smith," he said blandly.

Jason raised an eyebrow and glanced at Laura. She understood what he wanted, an explanation and fast. Usually when an operative stood in conversation for very long, it was because they were suspicious of something. How could she explain she was more interested in this man on a personal level than because of any suspicions?

"Tal is visiting from England. He met McNab for the first time tonight." Laura knew she should have gotten a last name by now, as well. She was not doing her job. She wasn't here to flirt with a stranger, but to make sure the man wasn't a cat burglar out to lift jewels from all the women in the place.

"Jason Abernathy."

The men shook hands.

"Will you be in San Francisco for long?" Jason asked.

"Not too long. I'm here on business. As soon as it's concluded, I'll return home," Tal said easily. A hint of amusement lurked in his eyes.

"We should circulate," Jason said to Laura.

Tal looked at her. "I thought you came alone."

"She came with me," Jason said.

"He asked if I was with anyone, I said no. Your giving me a ride isn't quite the same thing." Laura didn't want Tal to think she was dating Jason. Yet she couldn't explain why she was really here.

Jason looked at her, then at Tal. "She came with me," he repeated.

"Only because you offered to drive. Goodness, it's not a date or anything," Laura said, trying to laugh it off, but feeling embarrassed Jason was making such a big deal about it. "See you," she said to Tal and led the way toward the sliding doors that gave way to the wide balcony.

When they were out of hearing, she glared at Jason. "You didn't have to be so obnoxious."

"We're working. If you want to pick up some guy, do it on your own time. How do you know he isn't some con artist? Seems odd to me some foreigner shows up at a fund-raiser for a California state senator. Doesn't it you?"

"Maybe. I don't know. He came with a friend—Earl Rogers. When you get the chance, take some photos. We'll see if we can find out more about him at the office tomorrow. In the meantime, I have the name of his friend. Maybe I can figure out which one he is and ask him some questions."

"Great, and if they're a team, they'd cover for each other."

Laura sighed in exasperation. "Not everyone we don't personally know is a crook."

"Maybe." Jason looked around as if he didn't trust a soul. "I'll touch base with you in little while. Just try to keep your mind on business," Jason said.

Tal watched the two of them walk away. He'd pulled some strings with local contacts to discover information on Laura Toliver. She was a security operative for Beatty Security. Tonight she was undoubtably working, which explained why Yuusuf wasn't present. He'd taken a bold chance that his cousin might show up, but so far there was no sign of him. Tal really didn't think American politics held much appeal for his cousin, unless the candidate was tall, blond and about twenty-five.

Laura Toliver was not what he expected. Granted the newspaper photo had captured her looks, but not that sparkle in her eye, or the way her entire face became animated when she talked.

Her acting skills could use some work. A blind man could have told how annoyed she was with Jason when he interrupted their tête-à-tête.

A woman like that, surrounded by beauty and wealth at all her assignments, must covet the same jewels she guarded. No wonder she saw Yuusuf as her meal ticket out of working and into the glamorous lifestyle she now only saw from the periphery.

He had detected definite interest on the woman's part. Was it his Italian suit? The gold Rolex watch? Obviously she recognized the fruits of money when she saw it. How could she not be interested in a man who could outbid her current suitor and lavish attention and trinkets on her?

He'd made the first step. His choreographed plan would unfold as he intended over the next few days. With any luck, he'd be home in a week or two.

Looking for Earl, he found him near the canapés. Trust his old Eton friend to head for the food. Earl had been surprised when Tal contacted him. They hadn't kept in close contact over the years, especially after Earl had left England for a position in California. Tal had wrangled an invitation to this evening's event for the sole reason of meeting Laura. When Earl had expressed suspicion that Tal wanted to go, he explained he wanted to meet a certain woman. Earl was a romantic at heart and saw this as the start of a great love story.

"I'm heading back to the hotel," Tal told him. "The time change is catching up with me."

"I thought you'd be too tired to last the night. Good showing for Patrick, don't you think? He'll go far. After a couple of terms in the state senate, he'll be ready for Washington," Earl said proudly.

"The equivalent to one of your own MPs," Tal said, knowing Earl was an avid Labor Party member and loved debating the pros and cons of any major issue.

"You find that girl?" Earl asked, looking around.

"I did. I appreciate your help. If anything develops, I'll let you know."

"Just ask me to be your best man."

Earl was departing in the early morning for two weeks in Japan. The timing couldn't be better as far as Tal was concerned. He'd received his help and didn't have to play a part in front of his old friend. By the time Earl returned, Tal expected the situation with Yuusuf to be wrapped up and settled.

Laura made the rounds, speaking with several people she knew, being introduced to others, without giving away her true role in the evening's festivities. Most people there were too full of themselves to care to delve into her career. Once she'd made the rounds again, she looked for Tal. She'd like to continue their conversation, even if Jason didn't approve. He wasn't her boss.

But she didn't see the exciting stranger. The evening became tedious after that. She could hardly wait until it ended so she could get home to relive every moment she'd shared with Tal.

She smiled at the humor she'd recognized in his eyes when he told Jason that last name. She knew it was false. Why had he given it? Probably to annoy Jason. She hoped that was the reason and not that he was a con man toying with them.

By the time she was in bed, though tired, Laura was too keyed up to sleep. She had to trust her instincts and they did not indicate the man was a thief. He looked at her directly, with no hint of dissembling. When he had, she'd felt a spark deep inside as if a question was asked and answered.

Was she getting interested in him beyond the casual friendship she enjoyed with other men? If she weren't careful, she'd fall for Jenna's love-at-first-sight theory.

Daydreaming was well and good, but she wanted to know more about him and had no idea how to locate him. Maybe she'd call Earl Rogers herself in the morning and ask to speak to his guest. If Jason hadn't interrupted, would they have exchanged phone numbers and made arrangements to meet again? She fell asleep imagining a dozen ways she could see him again.

Laura didn't like Wednesday night events because it

meant even if she was up late, she was expected in the office on time. There were reports to file, people to research and other aspects of the job that went on regardless of the amount of sleep she wanted. And sleep had been in short supply because of her thoughts about Tal.

She'd finished writing her perceptions about the evening and wondered how differently Jason's report would read. One of the reasons some events had more than one operative was because of the different insights they brought. No two saw everything the same.

Take Tal for instance.

She had run Earl Rogers's name through the various databases, as well as Tal Smith's. Earl was from England, worked at a financial firm in the city and lived modestly in a flat in Pacific Heights. For Tal Smith, she found nothing.

Feeling a bit foolish, she called Earl's number. An answering machine responded.

"I'm off to Japan for two weeks. If you need me, call the office, they can reach me."

She hung up. Didn't the man know telling anyone who called he'd be gone was an open invitation to burglars? Though if he lived in a high-rise security building, it probably didn't matter.

It proved a dead end for finding Tal, however.

Giving up she turned her attention to business. They had been two people who met for a moment. It was too bad she wanted more. He'd seemed attentive enough during those few minutes, but maybe he acted that way with everyone. She had no way of knowing if he felt that special attraction that had flared so quickly for her.

Was it love-at-first-sight as she and Jenna had discussed? How unlucky if it were. She would probably never see the man again—except in her dreams.

By lunchtime, Laura was ready for a break. Her boss had called Jason and her in to discuss the McNab event, and future fund-raisers. Apparently McNab liked how they'd quietly handled the surveillance and wanted the agency to be a part of their campaign events.

"Good job to you both," Ben said. "Where possible, I'd like to send you two together again. If conflicts arise, I thought Aaron and Maggie."

"Good choices," Laura said.

Jason nodded.

When they left she asked him if he'd found out anything on Tal Smith.

"Nothing, which could or could not be suspicious."

"Right, he either has never been involved in a problem, or is too good covering his tracks to be traced," she said, wishing she knew for sure who he was.

Jason nodded. "He left shortly after we saw him and since no one had reported any problems, he most likely is just who he said he was. So if you're interested—go for it."

"We didn't get as far as that," she said. She was not going to admit to trying to find him.

But actually they ran into each other sooner than Laura would ever have expected. She left the building at lunchtime, wanting a quiet lunch, maybe a takeout sandwich from the deli to eat in the park. She headed down Montgomery Street toward the Bay. The sun was high in the sky, the air crisp and clear.

"Laura?"

She looked up into Tal's eyes. "Tal?"

Serendipity. She couldn't believe he was right in front of her. She smiled in secret delight. She'd been thinking about him all morning and now they'd run into each other again. Amazing.

"I just finished a meeting and was looking for a place for lunch. Any recommendations?" he said, stepping aside to allow a couple to pass. The sidewalk was busy with people on their noon break.

"I'm on my way to lunch myself. I work in that building," she said, gesturing to the high-rise that housed Beatty Security. Suddenly conscious of the slacks and plain top she wore, Laura wished she'd dressed up a bit more for work today. But she hadn't expected to see Tal again—at least not this soon.

"Have lunch with me. Are you on a short time schedule?" he asked.

"No, I'm flexible. I'd love to have lunch," she said, trying to remember if she put on lipstick recently.

"Where do you suggest? Something nice and quiet. I want to learn all about you," he said, reaching out to take her hand and tucking it in against his arm, holding it with his warm palm. And somehow Laura felt his touch was exactly right.

The first restaurant Laura recommended was too crowded. Tal suggested they try another one.

Hesitant because of the expense, she mentioned one tucked away right off Montgomery Street. Laura was worried about the cost; she'd always been careful to split the check with someone as wealthy as Jenna. She didn't ever want anyone to think she was taking advantage. But it was elegant, quiet and outrageously expensive—and consequently less likely to be crowded.

He agreed with no hesitation.

Seated at the linen-covered table a short time later, Laura hoped the choice hadn't been a mistake. The prices for a light lunch were amazing. Still, Tal seemed at ease in the surroundings. He asked her about her order, then gave them both to the waiter.

"Are you feeling acclimated to San Francisco time now?" she asked when they had ordered.

"I am. A good night's sleep was all I needed. I'll be on San Francisco time from now until I leave."

"And that will be when?" she asked. He hadn't said last night.

"As soon as my business is finished. Does your offer to show me San Francisco still stand?"

Her heart skipped a beat and then raced. He wanted to see more of her. Laura smiled, wanting to hug herself with joy.

"Sure does. I have to work tomorrow, but I'm free all weekend. Are you?"

"Yes. What do you recommend I see first?"

"Have you been here before?"

"Several times, but always on business. This time I shall take the opportunity to see more of your lovely city. And at least one of its inhabitants."

His smile warmed her heart. His dark gaze held hers. She wanted to reach out and touch him. She was falling for the man and she didn't even know his real name! But oh, how she enjoyed being with him. And the mystery added a certain cachet to their meetings.

"Actually the city is divided into different sections, like the financial district in which we are in now. There's the wharf, Chinatown, Market Street, Union Square, Nob Hill, Golden Gate Park and the Presidio. Then we have different residential neighborhoods, each with a unique feel." She was babbling. Abruptly she shut up.

"I put myself in your hands," he said.

Laura wished that could be a true statement. She'd love to run her fingers through that thick dark hair, feel the muscles of his shoulders, chest and arms. Touch those chiseled lips, feel the texture of his skin against hers.

Growing warm with her thoughts, she reached for her water glass, trying desperately to come up with a plan and to put a halt to the wild fantasies that raced in her mind.

"I'll make a list of things to see and you can tell me what appeals," she offered.

"Anything you suggest, I'm sure, will be fine. Money is no object."

She looked at him. Was he wealthy? Or was he planning to charge things to his company's expense account?

"You have a problem with that?" he asked, as if picking up on her hesitation.

"Just curious, I guess. Is this a company-sponsored trip?"

"Not at all. I'm on personal business. I have quite

enough money to spend however I wish," Tal said. "Do not consider that an obstacle when planning our itinerary."

Laura didn't think she would be planning anything that cost much. There was a great deal to see in the city for free. She loved to walk the hills, explore quiet gardens tucked off busy streets, or wander around Golden Gate Park, a huge expanse of natural green space that went to the Pacific. Sitting at the edge of the ocean held special appeal as well. Was Tal more inclined for elaborate dinners and more elegant pursuits? Or night clubs and dancing? If so, she'd be out of her element.

She hoped they'd find common ground. The attraction she felt was stronger than ever. She wanted to get to know him, have him learn about her. For a second, she realized she was feeling some of what Jenna felt for Yuusuf. Maybe there was such a thing as love at first sight. She'd certainly never felt like this before.

"Actually we don't need to spend a lot of money to see San Francisco. Some of the best aspects of the city are free," Laura said. She hoped he'd enjoy what she liked, and see San Francisco as she saw it, a beautiful city, full of interesting contrasts and intriguing people.

"You're the tour director. But if something appeals that costs money, don't hesitate."

Their food arrived and Laura asked Tal about his home.

"It's fairly large for a single man. Near the sea, I can go for a swim anytime I wish—if the weather cooperates."

"I imagine it's more cold than not in England, so you probably cherish weather warm enough to swim in. Isn't the water cold? I always picture England as under fog and rain," Laura said.

Tal inclined his head slightly. "England can be cold, but there are more sunny days than not, and the rain keeps the country green. I find San Francisco a bit cool for this time of year."

"It's the marine fog. Nature's air conditioner, we call it. Mark Twain once said the coldest winter he ever spent was a summer in San Francisco. But when the sun comes out, it's lovely."

"What section do you like best?" he asked. Tal watched Laura talk about the city. She obviously loved her home and he found himself intrigued with her despite himself. Her eyes shone with honest enthusiasm. She waxed poetic about different aspects of San Francisco, but he was more caught up by the woman herself than the places she described.

Her short hair framed her face, showcasing her expressive eyes. Her skin was almost translucent with creamy color and a hint of pink on her cheeks. She spoke about a park and the beach. He listened attentively wanting to learn more about her likes and wants to better fine-tune his plan.

He had lurked in front of her building for almost an hour, not wanting to miss her when she left for lunch. He'd planned their accidental meeting, and had been rewarded for his patience when he'd seen her leave the building alone.

Now to move forward. It was easy to be attentive,

easy to appear captivated by her enthusiasm. She surprised him when she hadn't immediately suggested an outing that cost money. Yasmine would have already figured out a way to discover his wealth. He pushed the thought away. Yasmine had been dead for four years. She no longer had any hold over him.

Maybe Laura was biding her time. He'd need to be careful. Of course, they'd only just met. She had no idea how much money he had, and wouldn't wish to jeopardize her connection with Yuusuf. He had to show her he would be more advantageous for her to pursue than his cousin.

Lunch was the first step. He'd recognized the restaurant when he'd seen it, and known it would be expensive. Let her see how lavishly he spent money. She'd change allegiance from Yuusuf to him before long. His cousin was not one to flaunt his wealth. But of course, the family riches were well-known—and some women could sense the opportunity. Too bad he couldn't cash in on that by revealing himself. But to make this work, he needed to keep his connection to Yuusuf silent.

Laura surprised him again when they left the restaurant and she headed back to work. He offered her an afternoon of fun, but she'd insisted she had to return to work. He walked her back to her building and asked her for her phone number. He had it already through his embassy contacts, but didn't want any questions to arise in the woman's mind. She gave it freely. Someone should warn her about being too open with strange men.

She asked where he was staying and he told her,

hoping she never called and asked for Mr. Smith. He was registered under his real name. But he gave her the room number, so she could bypass the switchboard if she ever called.

Upon his return to the hotel, he arranged with the concierge to send a bouquet of roses to Laura at work. He had a short time to win her away from his cousin and needed to set the stage.

Laura was surprised and delighted by the beautiful bouquet of pink and white roses that arrived before work ended. The card said simply, *Thanks for lunch.*

"Wow, some new guy in your life?" her friend Betty asked, eyeing the flowers. "These are gorgeous. You lucky girl."

"I am, aren't I. They're from a friend. A new friend," Laura said. The flowers were the prettiest she'd ever been given. Her feelings for Tal soared. She had never been sent flowers at work before. She liked the attention she received from the other girls.

When Laura had a moment, she phoned Tal at the hotel, asking for his room number. Hoping he was there.

"Thank you for the flowers," she said when he answered.

"Thank you for having lunch with me. I enjoyed it more than I expected." Wherever possible, Tal thought it easier to tell the truth. He was not used to a life of subterfuge. "I don't want to wait until Saturday to see you again. How about dinner tonight?"

"Oh. That would be great. Let me go home to change and I could meet you somewhere." She felt a warm glow. He wanted to see her again as much as she wanted to see him!

"Let me check with the concierge and get a recommendation. I can pick you up at your apartment," he said.

"I'll meet you. Call me when you find a place, or I'll suggest a couple." Despite her growing interest in the man, some basic precautions were needed. She wasn't revealing where she lived until she knew him better.

"I'll check with the concierge and call you back."

She made sure he had her work number before hanging up. She could hardly wait!

CHAPTER THREE

AT SEVEN, Tal arrived at the restaurant the concierge had recommended. It was very elegant and expensive. Exactly what he'd asked for. He'd told her he wanted to make an impression and she'd done her best to find him the right place. He had debated letting Laura suggest the restaurant. He was interested in knowing which one she might have recommended—the most expensive in town? Or might she have been more prudent? He needed to make sure she knew he had money and was more than willing to spend it on her.

As he waited, he wondered what she would tell Yuusuf about this evening. She had accepted his invitation too quickly. It was unlikely they'd made plans. He didn't think she'd throw over a sure thing for a mere possibility. Was there some way to make certain Yuusuf knew she was seeing another man?

The fog rolled in from the Pacific, cooling the evening air. The lights were starting to come on in the various high-rise office buildings. He checked his watch. He didn't have long to wait before Laura arrived in a cab. She was dressed in a conservative dark blue dress. Her short hair couldn't take long to style, but it looked tousled as if some man had just run his fingers through it. For a second, the thought produced a prick of jealousy. How intimate were Yuusuf and Laura? Tal found he really didn't want to think about that aspect of their relationship.

He was not really dating the woman, just luring her away from his cousin. He didn't really care how many men she slept with as long as Yuusuf wasn't one of them. He couldn't let his cousin get trapped.

"I hope I didn't keep you waiting," she said.

"Not at all. I just arrived. Shall we?" He escorted her inside. There was no view, just polished wood on the walls and heavy light fixtures. It reminded him of some of the English pubs he liked.

The chairs were leather and comfortable. The heavy silverware and delicate crystal shone beneath the subdued lights. Music played quietly in the background.

"Very nice," she said as she was seated.

"It received high recommendations with the wide selection of choices," he said as the maître d' presented the menus with a flourish.

"You haven't eaten here before?" she asked, glancing at the menu. It was in Italian, though she recognized the costs as being U.S. dollars—and many of them. She hoped he didn't mind spending a small fortune on dinner. On Saturday she'd make sure she kept their sightseeing inexpensive.

"I have not. The concierge at the hotel recommended the veal," he said softly.

When Laura looked up, Tal was watching her, not reading the menu.

"I like veal," she said, unable to tear her eyes away. She felt fluttery and feminine inside. And liked the feeling.

"Tell me, Laura, where did you grow up in San Francisco? I want to picture the house."

"I lived with my grandparents. My parents died when I was a child. Gramps and Gammy lived in Portrero Hill. We had a large flat, with a wooden balcony that overlooked the neighborhood. We didn't have much of a view. But I loved the neighborhood. My own apartment isn't far from where I grew up. What I remember most is how our place always smelled of cinnamon and vanilla. My grandmother was a wonderful cook and loved to bake."

"Was?"

Laura nodded, the pang at losing her beloved grandparents still strong. "Gramps had a stroke about five years ago. Shortly after he died, Gammy died as well. I always thought it was from a broken heart. They were the perfect couple. They'd been married a long time before my mother was born, I think they didn't expect to ever have a baby. So they weren't as young as other grandparents when I was growing up. But for me they were perfect. I miss them a lot."

When the waiter came for their order, Tal also ordered champagne.

"Are we celebrating?" Laura asked.

"Yes, the beginning of something special," Tal said. "I noticed you were drinking champagne last night. So you like it, right?"

"I love it." She hesitated a moment, longing to tell Tal that it had been ginger ale in her glass, but not wishing to spoil the mood—or explain exactly what she was doing at the McNab's fund-raiser—she didn't say anything.

"Tal, thank you again for the lovely roses. I was so surprised to get them. I wanted to take them home to enjoy, but couldn't carry them on the bus, so they're still at work."

"I'm glad you enjoyed them."

"A bit extravagant, but I love them."

He shrugged. "I can afford it. You gave me time you probably could ill afford, consider them a small token of my appreciation."

"How did you know where to send them?" she asked.

"I saw you speak to a woman coming out of the elevator as you were about to step in and asked her what company you worked for," he said, sidestepping the fact he'd known before he landed in San Francisco the name of the firm she worked for. He even knew what her job was, and how often she hobnobbed with San Francisco's society elite. Did it grate on her how extravagantly others lived when she was alone in the world and living in a small flat near Portrero Hill?

"Quite the detective. I'm impressed."

"Then I'm glad. It was my hope they would bring you pleasure," he said. And that it would bring her closer to fulfilling his plans.

Laura fell silent, wondering what else to talk about. Normally she felt at ease in most situations, but around Tal she felt off-center slightly, almost tongue-tied.

Their salads arrived and the awkward moment passed.

Tal proved to be an easy man to talk with she discovered as the meal progressed. He subtly asked questions about her life which secretly delighted Laura. He seemed as interested in her as she was in him. When she asked about his life, he didn't go on and on like some of her dates did. Telling her tidbits with brevity, he'd then turn the conversation back to her. Still, she cherished every morsel of information he revealed. He'd attended school at Eton, played with the local soccer team and loved sailing.

Dinner lasted far longer than she'd expected. It was growing late by the time she finished the last of the brandy he'd ordered after dessert.

"I need to get home and to bed," Laura said slowly, hating to end the evening, but it was already close to eleven.

"I have a very long day tomorrow," she said. "But we can meet early on Saturday. If the weather's good, would you like to explore Golden Gate Park?"

"I have a better idea, how about a balloon ride in the Napa Valley? I hear they are spectacular and not something I've done before. Have you?"

Laura knew about the large hot-air balloons that soared into the air, then drifted silently along the currents over the vineyards of the Napa Valley. If the day was clear, the far distant Sierra Nevada mountains could be seen.

"I've never done that," she said, knowing her smile held delight. "I would love to." *Especially with you.*

"I will make the arrangements. Shall I pick you up at six?"

"In the morning?" She had hoped to sleep in in the

morning, but she'd stay up all night and the next day, too, to spend a day with Tal.

"The balloons take off shortly after dawn. Before the day gets too hot. Bring a warm jacket. According to the brochure, it can be cool at the upper heights."

After Tal settled the bill, he escorted her out. Speaking with the valet parking attendant, he escorted Laura to the curb to wait. She shivered slightly in the fog, feeling cool after the warmth of the restaurant.

"Cold?" he asked. Without waiting for her answer, he slipped off his suit jacket and placed it around her shoulders. The warmth from his body enveloped her. His scent filled her nostrils.

"I was, but not now. Thank you. I should have brought a jacket. But it was warmer earlier in the evening." She snuggled in the warmth. "Aren't you cold?"

"No. Don't forget to bring one on Saturday."

A long, white stretch limousine pulled up in front of them. The driver quickly got out and came round the back to open the door.

"This is yours?" Laura asked in surprise. She'd thought he'd asked the valet parking attendant to summon a cab. Or to retrieve a rental car. She hadn't expected such luxury.

"While I'm in San Francisco," Tal replied.

Laura got into the luxury car and settled back on the leather seats. It was like sitting on the most comfortable chair she'd ever known. What fun. She'd never ridden in a limousine before, excitement rippled through her.

Tal got in beside her. "You'll have to give the driver directions to your place," he said.

After the enjoyable dinner they'd shared, and the background information exchanged, Laura's worries about telling Tal where she lived were gone. She quickly told the driver how to get to her apartment building, wondering what the street would look like to Tal. It was not at all opulent, just a nice working-class community. She lived only a few blocks from where she'd grown up. None of her neighbors had limos. What would they think when they saw this one?

When they reached her apartment building, Tal got out and walked her to the big glass door that led to the lobby. She shrugged out of his jacket, reluctant to return it.

"Thank you."

"Shall I see you up?" he asked, hooking it over his shoulder.

"That's okay. Thank you for a lovely evening. I really enjoyed myself."

"The pleasure was mine," he said, taking her hand and brushing his lips across the back. He then turned it over and kissed her wrist.

Laura felt her heart skip a beat. His bent head was so close it was all she could do to refrain from reaching out to run her fingers through the thick dark hair. Her heart pounded in her chest.

"Until Saturday," Tal said.

For a moment she thought he'd kiss her, but he smiled and stepped back.

She turned, opened the lobby door with her key and went inside. When she turned at the elevator, she saw him still standing there, watching her—almost brooding. Did he hate to say good-night as much as she did? Closing her eyes when in the elevator, she could see him clearly. Imagine him leaning closer and kissing her.

Her phone was ringing when she reached her door. Quickly unlocking it, she ran for the phone, shutting the door more forcefully than needed. She hoped she hadn't wakened any neighbors.

"Hello?"

"Where have you been?" Jenna asked. "I've called at least a dozen times."

Laura glanced at the answering machine. She had five new messages. Were they all from her friend?

"Or once or twice," she said, kicking off her shoes and sinking on the sofa.

"Okay, when you didn't call back, I tried again."

"I was out to dinner. Just got home. Jenna, I think it's happened."

"What?"

"I think I've found Mr. Right. See, I am open enough to recognize him when he arrives."

Jenna squealed. "Who is he? Where did you meet? What's he like? When do I get to meet him? How do you know?"

Laura smiled in sheer happiness. "There's something so special about being with him. He's tall, dark, absolutely gorgeous. He has the nicest manners and can talk about almost everything. At least it felt as if we talked about everything tonight. He's from England and has the most fabulous accent. I could listen to him talk forever."

"England. Is he visiting, or does he live here?"

"He's here on business. I hope he wants to spend every free moment with me. We had lunch together, then dinner."

"Oh, Laura, if he's here for a short time, he's just whiling away the hours. Don't fall for someone you can't build a relationship with," Jenna warned.

"Who says we can't. Maybe I'll end up going to London." She didn't want her happiness dimmed by cautionary be-carefuls, even from her best friend.

"I'd tell you what you're always telling me, be careful."

"You know me, I'm cautious and calm, a regular girl. But when I'm with him I feel fascinating. And feminine. When he looks at me with those dark eyes, I just about melt."

"Has he kissed you yet?"

"Sort of."

"What's that mean?"

"He kissed my hand." And wrist, but for some reason Laura felt that was too intimate to share. She rubbed her wrist against her cheek, feeling Tal's warm lips warm again. She had never had an evening go so quickly. Hoping she could capture each moment with him, she began to tell Jenna from the beginning.

"He sent me roses this afternoon," she said.

"Okay, sounds like my kind of guy. What else?"

"We're going out on Saturday—to a hot-air balloon ride in Napa."

"Oooo, I'm liking this guy more and more. Not your ordinary kind of date. Sounds like he likes you, too."

"I believe so. Oh, Jenna, what if this is the real deal? What if I'm falling in love at last. I thought I'd be forever single. I've wanted to be part of a couple for so long. To be really loved and cherished for myself. To finally belong to someone."

"I want you to have that, too. Did I tell you I'm taking Yuusuf home to meet my parents this weekend?"

"No. Are you that serious? That sure?"

"I'm sure. I think he loves me. He says he does. How does one ever know except to take the chance, trust in the other person and go for it?"

"Sounds like a winning plan to me." That's what she was doing, wasn't it, trusting in the future, embracing the special feelings she had for Tal. She wanted to hug them to herself in joy.

"Me, too. Anyway, I called Mom and Dad today and they invited us this weekend. Will we see you tomorrow night at the art showing for Jules Renault?"

"Yes. I'm working with another operative. We were told there would be more than five hundred people there. Do you think so?"

"No, I suspect that's how many invitations were sent out and the gallery's owner is hopeful. But I bet only about half show up. Yuusuf and I will be there early. I have another party I want to make, so we may cut out early."

"I'll be the one in black, circulating with ginger ale. Oh, did I tell you we had champagne at dinner? To celebrate what may become something very special," Laura said, remembering every word Tal had said, every gesture.

"You'll have to fill me in tomorrow. Bring him to the showing. I can't wait to meet him. And have Yuusuf meet him. Can't hurt to get a man's opinion."

"Oh, yeah, like this guy's got ulterior motives on

my salary! Anyway, I can't bring him while I'm working. There will be other times we can get together. Will you be gone all weekend?" Laura's parents lived in Monterey, about a three-hour drive from San Francisco.

"We'll be home Sunday evening. I'll call you when we get back."

"I hope everything goes well."

"I'm a little worried about Dad's reaction, he still thinks of me as his little girl. But you're the one I'm really concerned about. You're a babe in the woods around men. Watch it, while I'm gone. Don't get in over your head," Jenna cautioned.

Laura hung up, too excited and happy to let Jenna's warning dampen her mood. She'd had a fabulous evening, returned home in a limo and would be seeing Tal again on Saturday. She could hardly wait!

Tal settled back in the limo and idly watched the city lights as the driver returned to the hotel. The evening had gone exactly as planned. It was nice to know he could foresee the future so well. She was becoming captivated by his attention. He had to make sure he continued to make her aware of his wealth, without seeming to brag. She was smart, but he had the advantage. She didn't know he was out to wreck her scheme to capture his cousin. How disloyal she proved. Or was it some ploy to make Yuusuf jealous? Still, dinner with him tonight, all day Saturday. If Yuusuf found out, would he become disillusioned, or rationalize the situation? He was much more likely to compromise than Tal was.

When Tal reached the hotel, he dismissed the driver until Saturday morning. He would not need his services on Friday. While he had things he wanted to do, he could do that without the limo. That was just to impress Laura.

Saturday, he planned to pull out all stops to impress her. The question was how to convince her to turn away from his cousin without making any commitment or promises she could use to make a scene. If she *imagined* there was interest, *imagined* there was a future between them, that was hardly his fault.

But he made no promises to any woman. Not since asking Yasmine to marry him. He had lived up to his marriage vows, but in the end, it had almost destroyed him. He liked his life the way it was.

Though, for a moment, he felt a wave of anticipation for Saturday. He had never ridden in a hot-air balloon. It would be a new experience for them both. How would she react to the day? Saturday night, he'd take her to dinner and dancing. Sunday sailing on the Bay. What else would sweep her off her feet? An elegant dinner au deux? Lavish gifts at every occasion?

Jewelry, of course. That went without saying. All women coveted jewels. He'd have to see about getting her a trinket or two. Nothing extravagant, but enough to keep her hungering for more.

Tal dismissed Laura from his mind as he entered his room. It was too late to contact his office in Tamarin, but he would check email and the reports he asked his assistant to send. He could get a lot of work accomplished before turning in.

* * *

Friday evening Laura dressed in one of her serviceable black cocktail dresses. This one had a flowing skirt with a secret pocket for carrying miniature cameras or recorders, as the job demanded. She looked happy as she studied herself in the mirror. The sparkle in her eyes was from thinking about Tal all day. And knowing in just a few hours, she'd see him again. Tomorrow couldn't arrive early enough for her! She wished she'd told him about the art show. He could have stopped by. Maybe he liked discovering new talent.

No difficulties were anticipated for the showing, but she and Jason would have to be prepared for anything, which meant she had to stop thinking about the new man in her life and concentrate on business. It really wouldn't do to have him there, much as she longed to see him.

The evening proved to be routine. Laura mingled with people she recognized, listened to comments about the work of the artist being displayed. She didn't care for modern art, and the squares and squiggles meant little to her. Sea scenes were her favorites, or English country garden paintings. Monet was a personal favorite. However, she was not at the event to comment or complain, just to keep things under surveillance and report on anything or anyone suspicious.

"There you are," Jenna said, coming up and giving her a hug. Yuusuf was at her side, smiling.

"Hello," he said, offering his hand.

Laura shook hands briefly and smiled at her friend. "You two just get here? I thought you were coming earlier."

"We went to dinner first. And we're not staying

long. I want to go to the Culbertsons' party. What looks good?"

"These paintings don't do much for me, what do you think?" Laura asked Yuusuf.

Yuusuf glanced around and shrugged. "I leave the acquisition of artwork to those who know it. I'm only here because Jenna wanted to attend."

"Mr. Fontenrose is an old friend of my parents'," she explained, naming the gallery owner. "I'm here in their stead. Maybe I'll quickly check out the paintings, make sure he knows I came, and then we can blow this joint."

"I'll wait here with Laura," Yuusuf said.

Laura smiled at her friend. "I'll watch him for you,"

Yuusuf laughed. "I'll be fine on my own, but feel free. Go on, Jen, I'll be here when you're ready to leave."

Jenna waved and started around the gallery, stopping in front of some of the paintings and studying them, passing others quickly.

"I hear you two are going to them," Laura said.

"I am honored to be asked to meet them. Maybe I should arrange to take her to meet mine."

Laura was astonished. "Are you serious?"

"Do you not know how much I care for Jenna?"

"She could get hurt, you know. Just because she talks a good talk doesn't mean she's not fragile inside."

"She's not as fragile as you think, but—" he leaned closer as if to convey a secret "—if she were, she'd have nothing to fear from me. I plan to marry her."

Just then a photographer from the newspaper snapped their picture. He'd been taking photos all night and Laura hardly noticed the flash. She was too surprised by Yuusuf's revelation.

He smiled and the flash went off again. "But don't tell her. I want to ask her myself when I think the time is right."

"My lips are sealed." Laura was happy for her friend. Jenna seemed so in love with Yuusuf. And Laura knew just how she felt. She was falling in love with the most exciting man she'd ever met. At the same time it scared her, it also thrilled her that there was so much they didn't know about each other. And so much to work out. But Laura knew love was a special gift—once bestowed worth any sacrifice.

All her life she'd hoped for someone like Tal. At last she'd found the one man in the world for her. How could a woman be so lucky?

CHAPTER FOUR

TAL crumbled the early edition of the newspaper in his hands and threw it across the room Saturday morning. The limo was picking him up in ten minutes. Once again Yuusuf and Laura were on the front of the Life-Style section of the paper. If his grandfather saw it, he would definitely question how effective Tal's plan was.

He should have insisted on seeing Laura last night, but would she have refused? Probably. Yet she'd agreed to spend today with him. What had she told Yuusuf? Tal wondered if his plans for dinner this evening and a sail tomorrow would not happen because of a prior commitment to Yuusuf.

How could he make sure Laura chose him and repudiated Yuusuf? He looked at the small box on the table. He'd bought a gold bracelet with a small hot-air balloon charm. He would give it to her today. Add a charm each time they did something together. She'd be able to recognize immediately the diamonds and sapphires on the balloon, the quality of the gold bracelet. Soon she'd want more and more charms to increase the value of the bracelet. Then there'd be the hints for earrings to match.

Maybe a necklace. He knew what to expect. Yasmine had taught him well. He forced the memories back. No matter, it was all but a trifle to free Yuusuf from a mistake he'd always regret.

It was time to leave. He put the bracelet in his jacket pocket. He had to do all he could to captivate Laura this weekend—and cut Yuusuf out without the possibility of his regaining the lady's favor.

When the limo pulled to a stop in front of Laura's building, she came right out from the lobby. Obviously she'd been waiting for him. Tal smiled as the driver went around the back to open the passenger door. Tal climbed out to greet her. Was she that anxious to start the day, or was there something, or someone, she didn't want him to see in her apartment? His curiosity arose. He'd suggest a catered dinner one evening to make sure he could examine her apartment. It would give him more information about her which he hoped he could use to get into her good graces.

"Good morning," she said, her eyes bright.

"Good morning, you must have had a good night's rest, you look beautiful," he said deliberately, knowing she had to have been up late at the party with Yuusuf.

"I could hardly sleep in anticipation of today. I'm so looking forward to the balloon ride," she said with a happy smile.

Cynically Tal knew the real reason she'd hardly slept. He said nothing however, just waited while she slipped into the limo. He sat beside her and in only a moment, they were threading their way through the early

morning San Francisco streets on their way to cross the
Bay Bridge and on to Napa.

"Coffee?" Tal asked, gesturing toward the small
bar in front of them. A carafe of hot coffee rested on
the surface, two warmed mugs next to it. Cream was
in the small refrigerator and sugar in the gleaming
silver bowl.

"How delightful. Would you like some?" she asked.

"Yes."

She poured the fragrant coffee into the mugs.
"Cream or sugar?"

"I prefer it black."

"Me, too," she said, sitting back and handing him one
of the mugs. She sniffed the beverage and smiled. "It
always smells better than it tastes." She sipped and
smiled at him again. "Delicious."

"We'll have an al fresco breakfast when we arrive.
But this will tide us over," Tal said, longing to ask what
she and his cousin had done last night, but refusing to
even give a hint he suspected she was involved with
another man. He had to be careful in this wooing, until
she broke it off irrevocably with his cousin.

The ride was pleasant. The sunshine was diffused by
the tinted windows. The traffic light so early on a
Saturday that the driver made good time.

Tal soon had Laura talking about places she'd like
to visit, given time and money enough.

"Paris, I think. Doesn't everyone want to go to Paris?
And I'd love to see New Zealand. The pictures I've
seen of different places in that country are so spectacular. And Norway. The fjords are amazingly beautiful."

"Take in one country on each of your vacations," he suggested.

"There's still a lot to explore in my own country. I wish I had lots and lots of money. Then I wouldn't have to work and could travel all the time," she said wistfully. "But I content myself with travelogues and the occasional vacation trip someplace nearby."

"Would you like to see London?" he asked. Maybe a quick trip there together would alienate his cousin. It would be no more trouble than his coming to San Francisco.

"Of course! That almost goes without saying. To walk where kings trod, how cool would that be?"

"Other locations?" he prompted, suddenly curious as to whether she'd ever want to visit his part of the world.

"Maybe Spain or Italy, where I could bask on the shores of the Mediterranean Sea."

"North Africa has beautiful beaches," he commented.

"Egypt would be fantastic to visit, for the history alone."

His country had its share of history as well, but he wouldn't mention that. She'd know all about Tasimin from Yuusuf and any mention would immediately raise flags.

Before they ran out of conversation, they arrived at the staging area for the hot-air balloons. Tal felt curiously relaxed. He had to remind himself what the mission was and not fall to her charms. He began to understand why Yuusuf was attracted to this woman. She had an air about her that was appealing and innocent. She looked as if she loved life and found enchantment in even the mundane.

The bustle of activity belied the early hour. The sun

was already over the edge of the horizon, the air warming. Large, colorful splotches of silken material covered the field, in the early stages of being filled with the hot air that would elevate them high above the earth.

The sound of the fire nozzles was louder than expected. Tal got out of the car and held the door for Laura. She looked at the scene with amazement.

"There must be a couple of dozen balloons," she said. Two were halfway filled and looked like slightly deflated giant party balloons struggling to rise from the ground. Several were still quite flat. One was already upright but not yet tugging on the restraints. The primary colors and designs delighted the eye.

"Come." Tal led the way to the large tables to one side. Breakfast was already being served, prepared on huge wood-burning stoves set up in the field. The smell of bacon and sausage filled the air. Two men flipped pancakes, others stirred eggs in huge pans. One man withdrew hot biscuits from a Dutch oven. Several couples sat at the long tables, enjoying the meal.

The tables surprised Laura with their linen cloths and ornate silverware, lovely china plates and silver pots of coffee and tea. How elegant.

"This is amazing," Laura said as Tal gave his name to a hostess who quickly seated them at one of the long tables.

While they were eating, another hostess came over to get their names.

"You'll be in the red, white and blue balloon over there." She pointed to one of the balloons which was already inflated and looked ready to depart. "No rush.

As soon as you finish, let me know and I'll take you over." She glanced at her clipboard. "You also have lunch catered. It'll be in the basket." She then moved on to the next couple.

"Lunch in the air?" Laura asked.

"I thought it might be enjoyable. Or we can wait until we land."

"I don't believe I've ever had such an extravagant date. This is so much fun!"

He nodded. It didn't hurt to enjoy himself while moving his plan forward. For minutes at a time he could forget her mercenary goal and enjoy Laura's company. She was not as accomplished as Yasmine had been, lacking a certain amount of sophistication with her wide-eyed appreciation of everything. Yet it was refreshing in a way to have someone enthusiastic about an outing. He had not spared time for frivolous pursuits in ages. Yasmine had never wanted to share his sailing or other outdoor activities. Her love had been for shopping. So far Laura had not suggested that. But there was time for her true colors to come out.

Laura was having the best time of her life. Everything was perfect, from her escort, to the breakfast al fresco, to the prospect of spending a couple of hours floating high above the earth, just Tal and her. And the balloon driver. For a moment she wished they could have been alone, but of course neither of them knew a thing about guiding a hot-air balloon. She almost pinched herself to make sure she wasn't dreaming. Never in her wildest imagination had she dreamed of such an extravagant outing.

Tal took her hand when they left the table to follow the hostess to the balloon. Laura felt tiny surrounded by the colorful balloons, now inflated and tugging on their ropes. The geometric designs were bright with primary colors. The rattan baskets, or gondolas as she remembered they were called, were dark and gleaming. The blasts from the propane burners heating the air in the balloon envelope sounded like heavy static, blowing fiercely.

"This is Don, he's your pilot," the hostess said when they reached the red, white and blue balloon.

"Great to have you with us," Don said, shaking Tal's hand. "Let's get aboard and we'll be off."

In only minutes, the tethering ropes were released and the balloon began its slow accent. The burners gushed for a moment, then Don cut them off and silence reigned. Steadily the balloon rose and soon began drifting toward the rising sun. Below them the people on the field grew smaller. Acres of vineyards spread out in every direction like a very neat carpet. Surrounding the large Napa Valley were the mountains that appeared faint silver outlines in the early morning light.

"This is fantastic," Laura said softly. She looked at Tal. "Thank you for bringing me."

"My pleasure," he said. He reached for her hand and pulled her closer. Together they looked out over the view. The gondola sides came to about chest height. No fear of tumbling out. The burners were overhead and from time to time Don triggered the jets to keep the air in the balloon hot. When the burners were not firing, it was silent and quiet as the balloon drifted in the wind.

"I shall remember this all my days," Laura said

softly. The morning was perfect, as special as the man at her side. Her fingers gripped his as she relished the feel of his palm against hers, his fingers tightening in response. She was falling in love. She hardly knew the man, yet she felt safe with him. Felt a connection she'd never felt with anyone else. Felt an excitement that made everything seem bright and beautiful. It was as if she saw the entire world differently. Dare she hope Tal might come to feel the same for her?

What if he didn't? What if this was just a pleasant interlude while he visited San Francisco.

For a moment Laura felt panicked. She didn't want this time with him to ever end. Yet he'd given her little evidence that his feelings were involved. If he left without wanting to see her again, she'd feel bereft. She'd only met him a few short days ago, yet couldn't imagine not having him in her life now. Love at first sight didn't only happen to one of a couple, did it? She felt a shiver of apprehension. She shook it off. She would not let anything put a damper on their day.

He released her hand and put his arm around her shoulder, leaning closer, and pointing out a landmark in the distance. "Do you see it?" he asked.

She nodded, her heart pounding. She wanted to turn her head slightly, have her lips touch his, take a kiss and forget about the pilot also sharing the gondola with them.

"It's so beautiful," she whispered.

He didn't respond until she turned and looked at him. His face was so close she could feel his breath brush her cheeks. His dark eyes stared into hers. "I think you are so beautiful," he said and lowered his head for a kiss.

It was more than Laura ever dreamed. She forgot about the pilot. To her there were only two people alive, Tal and herself. Floating high above the ground, being swept away by his kiss, it was heavenly. She felt she could float away without the balloon.

He turned her until they were face-to-face, breast to chest, and enveloped her into his embrace, deepening the kiss. Time stood still as the erotic feelings surged through her like the hot air of the burners. Every cell in her body was attuned to Tal, to the feel of his lips against hers, his muscular body pressed against hers. The riotous sensations that fired passion flaring.

The blast of the propane jets jarred her back to reality. Pulling back a bit, she gazed up into his eyes, breathless.

"I shall never forget this day," she said softly.

"Nor I," Tal said, kissing her gently.

By the time they returned to earth, Laura suspected Tal was feeling as strongly about her as she felt for him. They were in love. Where would this wondrous state take them? Could she, as she'd told Jenna, move to London, start a new life there with this wonderful man?

Laura halfway expected the aftermath of the balloon ride to be anticlimactic, but it wasn't. The lunch was served by Don in lavish picnic style. A white tablecloth was spread on a thick blanket on the ground. A wicker basket full of picnic food also held china, crystal, silver and champagne.

Laura laughed when she saw it. "Champagne? At eleven o'clock in the morning?"

"A champagne picnic. Let me fill your glass, then have some paté with it. Lunch looks like a feast."

She would have been satisfied feasting her eyes on Tal but she dutifully accepted his offer of champagne and raised her glass when he filled his own.

"To us," she said recklessly.

He inclined his head slightly and touched the edge of his glass to hers.

They were alone on the blanket. Don explained he had to pack the balloon for transport back to the launch site. The ground chase crew would be arriving soon to take them all back to the staging area. He went to start the laborious job of folding the balloon while Laura and Tal ate.

Laura served their lunch on the elegant china and devoured the delicious cuts of meats and various cheeses. The paté was delicious. She discovered cut vegetables with a dipping sauce and even dark-chocolate-covered strawberries. She felt like she was in a movie or something. She'd never had such an elegant meal, much less a picnic.

"For not doing much this morning but standing around and looking at the scenery, I'm hungry," she said.

"You didn't eat much breakfast," Tal commented.

"I was too excited."

While they ate, they talked about the beauty of the valley they'd seen.

"I have something for you," Tal said when they finished eating. He reached into his pocket and withdrew a small box.

Laura put aside her plate and took the box when he offered it. Opening to a delicate golden chain bracelet with a small hot-air balloon charm dangling, she caught her breath. She lifted it gently from the velvet, her heart pounding.

"It's beautiful." Delicate and detailed, the balloon was red and blue, almost like the one they'd flown.

"A reminder of our day together," he said.

"You shouldn't have been so extravagant, but I love it. Put it on for me, please," she said, handing him the bracelet and holding out her arm.

He fastened it around her wrist, then took her hand and kissed the palm, closing her fingers over, as if to capture the kiss. "Your wish is my command."

"Thank you." Laura wished the day would never end. She couldn't remember ever being so happy.

As if reading her mind, Tal smiled, released her hand and asked her to dinner.

"It is short notice. You may have other plans," he said.

"I don't, but even if I did, I'd rather spend the evening with you." She knew she should be a bit more guarded about her emotions, but she'd never been in love before. She wanted him to know she liked spending time with him. What could it hurt?

"Perfect," Tal said, with a gleam in his eyes.

He took her home and promised to pick her up at seven. Laura dashed into her apartment and went to take a quick shower. Soon as she was finished, she took a nap. She'd been up late Friday night working, up early this morning. She didn't want to fall asleep at dinner because she was too tired.

Sleep came quickly, filled with romantic dreams of

Tal. When she awoke at six, she felt refreshed and looked forward to dinner with all the anticipation of a woman for one special man.

Dressing in a blue silky dress, she fingered her golden bracelet. The sparkling stones in the balloon glittered in the light. What a romantic gesture, she thought. What could she do to show him the day meant as much to her?

Just before seven, she grabbed a wrap and her small decorative purse, tucking her key inside. She was at the lobby door when the limo pulled up in front.

"Hold on," she admonished herself softly. "Don't rush out like you couldn't wait. He'll come to the door and you can walk out as if you just arrived."

Tal came to the lobby door, but before he could ring the bell, she opened the door and calmly walked out to meet him. So much for patience.

"Promptness is a virtue," he said gravely. "One I appreciate."

"You said seven," she replied as she got into the limo.

He took her to Fisherman's Wharf, to Buscallia's. Renowned for its excellent seafood choices, and preparation, it usually had a waiting list for weeks. How had he managed to get reservations on a Saturday night? she wondered as they went inside.

The far wall was entirely glass, with a spectacular view of the Golden Gate Bridge and the wispy fog beginning to drift in on the evening breeze. There were still sailboats on the Bay, and the tour boats could be seen, loaded with passengers who gazed with rapture at the San Francisco skyline.

"This way, sir," the maître d' said as he led them to a table for two immediately next to the windows.

"I believe the sunset will be spectacular," he said as he offered the menus with a flourish. "The fog won't come completely in until after dark. Enjoy your meal."

Laura stifled a giggle. "He sounded as if he arranged the sunset himself," she said.

"That would be an extra attraction if possible," Tal said. "What did you do since I last saw you?"

"Napped. I feel totally decadent," she said with a smile. *He had missed her!* "First the luxury of this morning's ballooning, then a nap, now dinner at such a wonderful restaurant. A person could get used to life like this."

He shrugged. "If one had money enough."

"Ah, the big stumbling block." She looked at the menu and debated her choices. She loved lobster, didn't have it often. If today was all about dreams coming true, she'd better stick with that.

"I'll have the lobster."

"I'll join you," he said, not even looking at the menu. He hadn't taken his eyes off her since they sat down.

She raised her wrist and let the bracelet dangle for a moment. "I don't know if I'll ever take it off," she said.

He reached into his pocket and pulled out another small box, sliding it across the table. "I want to take you dancing after dinner, so bought this at the same time I bought the balloon charm."

She opened the box to a dainty charm of a pair of dancing shoes, a small sparkling stone in the heel of each one. "Tal, you shouldn't have."

"I thought we'd build memories together and you'd have something tangible to remember me by."

Her smile faltered. "I'd rather have you," she said.

"I'm still here. I thought you'd like the charms."

"I do. But it sounds as if you are going away and I'll never see you again. I would hate that."

Tal had to give her credit for her acting. He'd been wrong, she was good. For a moment he could almost believe she meant it. As if anyone would miss a person they had met only a few days before.

He'd known she'd appreciate the charm. This one had diamonds in the heels of the shoes. The one he bought in anticipation of their cruise had a pattern of ruby sails in the boat. He'd give her that tomorrow when he took her sailing on the Bay.

He wondered how she'd explained her unavailability to Yuusuf. How long could she play the two men against each other? Yuusuf might believe anything, but Tal would push until she had to choose. For tonight, he might as well enjoy himself while he continued to make Laura think she was the new center of his world.

He didn't have to work hard at it, she was so blinded by greed, she'd see whatever she wanted. Did she realize how open she was? Accepting expensive gifts, hinting at travel plans. Did she expect him to whisk her away to London for a weekend? Or a shopping spree in Paris?

For a moment he toyed with the idea. How far would the woman go to try to snag a rich husband? He rather thought she'd hold out for a ring without giving of herself. It would be interesting to find out.

Laura gazed at the boats sailing by on the wind.

"I thought tomorrow we might go sailing," Tal said, noting the interest.

Her gaze swung to him. "On the Bay?"

"Or on the ocean."

She frowned. "Do you have a boat here?"

"No, my friend Earl has one. I've already asked if I can use it. The weather will be perfect. Come with me."

She studied him a moment. He wished he could read her mind. Watching her, tension rose a fraction. Had he pushed too far too fast? Was she doing something with Yuusuf tomorrow and was weighing in on which man to bet on? Before he could up the ante, she smiled.

"Thank you, I should love that," she said.

"I'll pick you up around ten, then."

She nodded, sipping from her water glass.

"Tell me what it is you do, Tal," she said when she carefully replaced the glass.

"I work with a cruise line, sailing primarily in the Mediterranean," he said. He didn't know how much she knew about Yuusuf's family and source of wealth. But he was hoping it was vague enough to keep speculation at bay.

"I can't imagine what you'd be doing here on business if you work for a cruise line firm in England."

"We have more than one office," he said. "Where better to attract customers than from the United States."

"What is your particular job?"

"I run the place," he said, with a touch of pride. He enjoyed his work. Besides, it was a shortcut to letting her know he had enough wealth to support her in the style she aspired to.

"Fantastic. I've never known anyone who even owns a sailboat, much less a cruise line. Will you be here long this trip?"

"I will be here as long as I need to be."

Laura smiled at the words.

"I shall look forward to seeing more of you," she said.

Cynically Tal knew he'd piqued her interest, set the hook. Was it time to begin reeling her in?

Dinner was served with a flourish. Laura ate the lobster with every evidence of enjoyment, despite the large bib the waiter insisted she wear to protect her clothes. Seeing Tal garbed in like bib was fun. They talked about San Francisco, which he had visited only twice before. Then they moved on to holidays they'd taken. His sounded more glamorous than hers, since she'd rarely been farther from San Francisco than Nevada. When he talked about skiing in Gstadd, or snorkeling in the British Virgin Islands, her eyes shone with excitement. She'd love to try everything he mentioned.

"Where is your favorite spot?" she asked.

He hesitated a moment, then shrugged. "Home."

"Mine is Lake Tahoe. It's especially lovely in late spring, when the snow still clings to the mountaintops, but the lower elevations have acres of wildflowers, and everything is still green. By summer, the grasses have dried to brown, the snow is gone and only the deep blue of the water contrasts with the dark green of the conifers. Still, I love it."

"We should go one weekend," he said. Maybe it

would suffice to take her there instead of London. Though she'd probably only see it as a warmup trip.

"If you haven't seen it, you should. It's a jewel tucked into the Sierra Nevada Mountains. There are also lots of casinos on the Nevada side of the lake if you're interested."

"Not particularly." Tal would rather gamble with his talents in business than waste money on machines or games designed to make the house the winner.

"Tell me about your job," he said.

Laura always kept a low profile about her work. She didn't want people to become self-conscious at events if they saw her, or discuss her role where the wrong person could overhear. And she was always just the tiniest bit suspicious when someone new in her life asked. Not that she need worry about Tal.

"I do a lot of background checks," she said vaguely. "Have you been sailing on the Bay before?"

"Never. Should be a new experience, like our balloon ride. What kind of background checks?"

"To make sure people are who they say they are. The balloon ride will forever be a favorite memory." And the kisses they'd shared.

"You check into financial ratings and things?" he persisted. Was that how she'd settled on Yuusuf?

"Among other aspects of a person's life. I think I'll skip dessert. I'm so full from dinner." She didn't want to talk about her job, but also didn't want to raise a red flag. Thankfully the waiter had been watching and came to clear her plate.

"Any dessert, coffee?" he asked.

Tal checked with her again but Laura shook her head.

When the man left, Tal reached out and took her hand. "The Palm Room was recommended as a place for dancing. Shall we?"

"I should enjoy that." Being held in his arms, moving to music, what a romantic night. And the ballroom was at the top of one of the larger hotels in San Francisco. She knew there would be a panoramic view of the city.

And so it proved. Laura was never sure how everything worked so perfectly, but it had. The music was romantic and designed to draw lovers together. The club was not crowded, yet full enough to have the buffer of anonymity. The city seemed to be spread out before them as if designed especially to make the night memorable. Even the drifting fog was wispy enough to merely blur the city lights, not smother them.

They ordered drinks when they'd been seated at the tiny table near the dance floor. Once the music started again, Tal rose and held out his hand for her. Laura felt like Cinderella at the ball. Moving easily into Tal's embrace, she was soon swept up in the magic of the evening.

Tal was an excellent dancer. He guided her so it seemed as if they'd been dancing together forever. With the music in her head, his hands holding her, Laura knew she had never had a better time. Dreamily she wondered what it would be like to go dancing every night with Tal. She couldn't imagine ever getting tired of being with him. He was interesting, entertaining and seemed determined to make sure she enjoyed herself at every turn.

The evening continued in a dreamy state. They didn't

need to talk much. For her part, Laura knew she didn't want to risk shattering the romantic mood with more mundane conversation. She hoped Tal felt the same.

Finally he asked her if she was ready to leave. It was late. She'd agreed, only because she knew she'd be seeing him again tomorrow.

When they reached Laura's apartment, Tal walked her up to the door.

"I enjoyed this evening," he said in that low sexy voice of his. "I'll see you in the morning, right?"

"Of course, what time?"

"I'll pick you up around ten. I thought we could sail out under the Golden Gate Bridge and along the coast for a short distance."

Laura had gone out on friends' boats a time or two, but never beyond the Bay. She was thrilled with the thought of doing something so exciting with Tal.

"Ten, then," she said.

He nodded, leaned forward and kissed her.

She almost melted. Her knees were decidedly weak. Kissing him back, she once again had the feeling time was standing still. Or she was still floating in a hot-air balloon high above the ground.

"Until then," he said, his eyes dark and mysterious, his voice husky.

Sleep came slowly, she had too many wonderful memories to relive from the evening and earlier.

She'd spend all day Sunday with Tal as well. Laura could hardly wait.

CHAPTER FIVE

THE morning was overcast with the marine layer of fog blanketing the city. Laura dressed warmly, knowing it would be even cooler on the water. She hoped the typical summer weather pattern wouldn't put Tal off. By noon the sun would have burned through the fog and the day would be beautiful.

Determined to show a little restraint, she decided not to go downstairs early, but wait for his buzzer on the outside door to let her know he'd arrived. There was such a thing as being too eager. In reality, she wished she could have had him come even earlier—had breakfast together.

She put on her charm bracelet, watching the little balloon sparkle in the light. She had the shoe charm on her dresser. She'd have to see about having it added to the bracelet. What a romantic man Tal was. Imagine wanting to hold on to memories in such a tangible way when they'd just met. Seemed like a long-range kind of outlook to her. Feeling giddy with excitement, she peered out the front window, hoping to spot the limo. The last few moments before ten seemed to drag by. She checked her watch a half dozen times.

Finally her vigil was rewarded, the limo turned onto the street. She stepped back from the window, wondering how long her heart would race at the mere thought of seeing Tal. She wanted to fly down the stairs to be at the door before he could ring. But she took a deep breath and waited for the buzzer announcing he was at the lobby door.

The knock on her door startled her. She went to open it and found Tal.

"How did you get in?" she asked, surprised.

"One of your neighbors was leaving as I arrived. She'd seen the car yesterday and figured it was safe to let me in, so she said. Are you ready?" He glanced beyond her into the small apartment.

"I am." Laura reached for her jacket. He looked wonderful wearing casual clothing. Of course, she felt definitely biased—she thought he looked wonderful in everything she saw.

Laura stepped into the hallway, closing the door behind her. She tested the lock, then smiled at him, her delight probably clearly evident. But she wasn't into playing games. She liked the man and didn't care that he knew it.

The limo quietly drove to the marina. Tal assisted her out and ushered her toward a slip down the pier. When they reached the boat, he lightly stepped aboard, holding his hand for her. She was a bit more cautious in stepping across the narrow expanse of water and onto the boat.

The sailboat wasn't as large as Laura had anticipated. Yet it was perfect for two. The sails were furled, the deck clear. Tal opened the small door to the cabin and disappeared inside.

"Just checking to see if our lunch arrived," he called.

Laura took a deep breath of the salty air. Gulls cried as they circled overhead. A few floated on the water. The fog kept the temperature cool, but she knew it would burn off before long.

"Nice friend you have, to let you use his boat," she said as Tal returned to the deck.

"Earl and I have been friends for years. He's welcome to use my boat when he's in England. Have you been sailing before?"

"Only a few times. I'm not an expert," she said.

"I am. I've been sailing since I was a boy. I've even participated in some races. Sit back and relax. This is a perfect boat for us. We'll have a great day."

Laura sat where he indicated, but relax she didn't. She watched with avid interest as he prepared to get underway. Once again Laura had the feeling she was being courted in the most romantic manner imaginable. She wasn't sure what she'd done to deserve such extravagant attention, but she cherished every moment.

Tal used the engine to move slowly through the crowded marina. The fog was damp and cool, the air tingling with each breath, unlike the sun-drenched Mediterranean he was used to sailing. He glanced at Laura. She looked as if she were having the time of her life. For a moment he wished he could take her at face-value. It would be nice to spend the day with a woman who had no agenda but to enjoy herself.

No wonder Yuusuf was taken with her. She looked radiant. How much longer before she would show her true colors to his cousin and he could end this farce? For a moment doubt surfaced. He hardened his heart against foolish sentimentality. Yasmine had shown him what women were like. He had to prove to Yuusuf that he needed to be more wary when women fawned over him. Money was a powerful attraction.

Cynically he glanced at Laura, wondering how hard it was to juggle two men at the same time—until she knew which would be the better choice. He had to dazzle her with his wealth and attention until she repudiated Yuusuf. He just hoped it was soon, before he became caught up in the charade he'd started and began to think there could be something between them.

Once free of the marina, Tal turned off the engine, raised the sails and settled near Laura, taking the wheel. The breeze was brisk and they moved swiftly through the water. She asked a dozen questions about sailing. Pointing out landmarks she recognized, she seemed enchanted to be aboard. He watched fascinated with her changing expressions. For a moment he wondered if he dare pursue her for himself. He could enter into a relationship fully aware she was only in it for the money. She would prove to be entertaining. The last couple of days had proved that.

He was in no danger of succumbing to her wiles. He knew better. He didn't believe in love. That was an emotion that always caught Yuusuf. A fanciful notion so prevalent in America. Sound values and shared commitment would suit a marriage better in the long run.

It could never work between him and Laura, he knew. Tal could not expose her as a fortune hunter to Yuusuf and then take up with her himself. His cousin would never forgive him. Family was more important than a pretty woman who intrigued him.

He set out to make the day perfect, to bring her that much closer to ending things with Yuusuf. Which would mean he'd be free to return to Tamarin and the work and life that he enjoyed.

Tal headed the boat toward the Golden Gate and the Pacific. Within the hour they had sailed beneath the towering bridge and out onto the gentle swells of the Pacific. Tacking northward, he kept the coast in sight. While an excellent sailor, this was new territory and he would just as soon stay in sight of land. He'd reviewed Earl's charts and had a definite destination in mind. The sun began breaking through the fog. In only a short time, they'd be bathed in sunshine, and hopefully warm up a bit.

"This is fabulous," Laura said, leaning closer.

"I'm glad you like it." He took her hand, lacing their fingers together and resting their linked hands on his thigh, while his other hand kept control of the wheel. He had found a quiet cove on the charts and wanted to anchor there for lunch. It would be another hour or so until they reached it. In the meantime, he had a role to play. And a cousin to save.

The cove he'd been seeking was formed by a spit of land that curved out like a fish hook. It was encircled on three sides by steep cliffs, towering redwood, pines and cedars growing at the land's edge. There was no beach to speak of, only the softly lapping water against the cliff base. The encompassing arms of land that sheltered the stretch of water, protected it from the trans-Pacific waves.

"This is enchanting," Laura said, as she surveyed the small cove. With the sailboat anchored, she truly felt alone in the world with Tal.

"Lunch?" Tal asked.

"Since you did all the work getting us here, I'll set up," Laura offered, jumping up. She fetched the picnic basket from below, opening it to wineglasses, china plates and silver utensils. She unpacked a linen tablecloth, which she spread on the narrow flat of the deck. Setting their places as if they were dining in a fine dining room, Laura then unpacked the food. Paté with crackers, a cold collation of meats and cheese, thick, crusty bread, fruit and a torte for dessert. And, of course, champagne. It was fantastic.

"I could get use to this kind of life," she said, when they were seated and began to eat.

"It wouldn't pale after a time?" he asked.

"I doubt it. But it's only a dream. I have to work for a living, as do most people. Wouldn't it be wonderful to be fabulously wealthy, travel the world and do whatever you wanted."

"Even fabulously wealthy people usually work to keep that wealth," Tal commented.

"Maybe. But I'd still love to have money enough to do whatever I wanted when I wanted."

"You like to travel."

"I wouldn't mind seeing some places I haven't seen before. Such as England," she said daringly.

Would he consider it a hint for an invitation? Did she mean for it to be?

"Maybe before you know it, you'll be traveling to places you always wanted to see," he said. He put down his plate and reached into his pocket.

"I have something for you," he said, pulling out a small jeweler's box.

Laura's heart jumped. Was he proposing?

He handed it to her. Frowning, she took it. If this was a proposal, he could be a bit more romantic about it. She didn't want to open a box and see a ring. She wanted fancy words of love and promise. She bit her lip, forcing herself to stop getting carried away. Lifting the lid, she saw a sailboat charm. The detail was amazing in a charm less than an inch in size. The sails glittered with rhinestones, the waves along the boat line were of blue stones. It was exquisite.

"Another memory for your bracelet," he said.

"It's darling," Laura said, happiness once again back in her heart. She and Tal had not known each other long enough to consider such a serious step as marriage. She knew that in her mind, just had a bit of trouble convincing her heart. As far as she was concerned, she would love him all her life.

She lifted the charm and held it to the sun. The reflected light was amazing. The blues so deep and true, the rhinestones glittered in every shade of the rainbow.

"I wouldn't need a charm to remember this day," she said. Leaning over, she kissed Tal. "But I shall cherish this memento. Don't keep buying me things, though. Just being with you is what I enjoy."

"Nicely said," he replied.

Laura was taken aback by the comment. Did that mean he thought she said the words but didn't mean them?

"I'm serious. I don't want gifts. Just your time, as much as you can spare while you're here."

"Surely you have other commitments, other people to see," Tal said. "If not, then consider all your free time spoken for. Spend it with me."

Her heart brimming, she nodded. "Now put this back in the box and keep it safe until we get home. I'd be afraid I'd lose it. Then I can put it and the shoes on the bracelet."

"Don't worry, I'll have them both affixed tomorrow."

Once lunch was finished, they leaned back against the bulkhead to enjoy the gently bobbing sailboat. The sun was high overhead but a cool breeze kept them comfortable. Laura wanted to know everything she could about the man who had captured her heart.

"Tell me everything," she said at one point.

He laughed and shook his head. "That would bore you to tears. You know the important things. I like to sail. I work for a shipping company. I like spending time with you."

"I've never been on a cruise ship," she said. "I've seen pictures of ones that sail from San Francisco. They look wonderful."

"One day I'll take you on a ship."

"Is working for the shipping company why you like to sail, or did you sail first and then look for a similar job?"

"Cruise lines are in no way akin to sailing. One's business, the other pure pleasure. I've been sailing since I was a boy."

"Where do you live in England?" she asked. "Do you have a house or a flat? Do you have a limo there, or is that just for us?"

He seemed to hesitate a moment, then nodded. "I have a flat in Knightsbridge. It's convenient to everything. Most of the time I use the underground or a cab to get around London. I do have a car to drive when I wish."

"And is your flat all modern and glass and chrome, or more traditional?"

"What do you consider traditional?" he asked.

"Not glass and chrome and leather," she said. "My place is decorated in early American, maple furniture, flower patterns on the fabric. I have some things from my grandmother that I display. It suits me."

"You said your immediate family is dead. Do you have aunts and uncles? Distant cousins?"

"Nope. No one, actually. I'm an orphan." Laura said it without pity. She'd been used to being alone for a long time. She often thought she would remain alone, until she met Tal. None of the men she'd dated over the years had ever set her to thinking of marriage and family and growing old together. But with Tal she could envision them making a life together. Supporting each other in their endeavors. And especially having children.

She'd love to have a little boy version of the man with her. Dark hair, dark eyes and enough charm to give all the little girls a run for their money. Or maybe a dark haired little girl who would wrap her daddy around her little finger. Would Tal like children? It seemed too personal and presumptuous to ask on such short notice.

"Do you like children?" she asked anyway.

He nodded. "I have a few nieces and nephews, children of my sisters and their husbands. When they visit, I enjoy spending time with them. Their view of the world is so innocent."

"I guess people lose that as we grow up. It's not as nice a world as I would like," Laura said. Times were hard with no family to call on for support. She had Jenna. Despite their differences in background and situations, they were best friends. She would be lost without her.

She had other friends, but none with the closeness or the history she had with Jenna. She wanted to talk to her friend about Tal. Conversely she also wanted to keep him a secret just a little longer. It made him seen more hers alone if she didn't tell all to Jenna. Was this how Jenna felt about introducing Yuusuf to her family? It opened a whole can of worms. She guessed introducing Tal to Jenna was akin to taking him home to meet her family. It would keep a little longer.

Besides, Jenna was so taken up with Yuusuf, she didn't have the time she once did for Laura. Now Laura understood it. She wanted to spend all her time with Tal. She dreaded having to go to work in the morning. When would she see Tal again?

"How much longer are you in San Francisco?" she asked.

"However long it takes."

"What takes?" Sometimes he could be so cryptic.

"The job I'm on," he said, flicking her a look.

Laura watched the coastline for a moment wondering at the bleak feeling that swept through. She knew he'd be leaving before long. Maybe he didn't feel the same for her as she felt for him. Love at first sight was uncommon, she knew. Still, if she felt so strongly, wouldn't he feel the same? She wasn't imagining the connection she felt between them.

"Come to dinner at my place one night this week," she said, offering an invitation she didn't know she was going to give. Time to see if this relationship would survive the normal mundane aspects of life. Being romanced with wildly extravagant things was one thing, but real life was more about day-to-day living. Maybe she was caught up in the glamor of the weekend, of their luxury dates.

Looking at Tal, she knew that wasn't the case. Still, she wanted to see him in the normal routine of her life. To see if she really could envision them together. She hoped it wasn't just a holiday fling, but a binding tie that would survive anything.

"When?"

"Wednesday. I have to work Thursday and Friday nights. So that would be best."

"I'd like that," Tal said.

It was late afternoon when they returned to Laura's apartment. She invited him to come up, he said he'd only come up for the charms and bracelet. He took them when she brought them to the door, kissing her gently and biding her farewell.

Once alone inside the apartment, Laura leaned against the door, holding on to the feel of him. It had been a special day. She was about to explode with de-light—dashing across the room, she was in time to see him get into the limo. She watched until the luxury car was out of sight.

He'd taken the bracelet to have the charms affixed, and would bring it back on Wednesday when he came for dinner.

Dancing around the living room, Laura was happier than she'd ever been before.

Stopping suddenly, she looked around. She had dusting and cleaning to do before she could show off her apartment for the first time to the man she loved.

The man she loved. She was in love. And so happy she was almost afraid. Was this what every woman went through when they fell in love? Wanting to be with the man every second, afraid so much happiness couldn't last. Not wishing to jeopardize anything that would spoil the perfection of the relationship.

She really needed to talk with Jenna.

She called her friend, knowing she was probably not yet back from the weekend at her parents' home. Laura left a message, impatient to hear from her.

It was almost nine o'clock when Jenna returned the call.

"How was the visit home?" Laura asked.

"It was terrific. Both my parents like Yuusuf. My dad spent part of Saturday alone with him, questioning him in detail, I take it, but Yuusuf was a good sport about it and at dinner, Dad said he was all right. High praise. But guess what? I'm engaged! After their talk, Yuusuf asked my father for my hand in marriage. Isn't that so formal and old-fashioned? But so romantic—especially since Dad said yes. And so did I!"

"Jenna, that's so wonderful. I'm happy for you! When will you get married?"

"We haven't set the date yet. I'm flying to Tamarin in another week or two to meet his mother and the rest of his family. I'm nervous. Do you think they'll like me?"

"What's not to like? They'll love you. Especially since you'll be making Yuusuf happy."

Jenna went on about the wedding, what she wanted for colors and decorations. Laura listened impatiently. She wanted to talk about *her* weekend. "Whew, I'm exhausted just telling you everything. I can't believe we'll be married this time next year," Jenna ended.

"I'm so happy for you."

"Thanks. I'll come by to show you the ring. You're not working tomorrow night are you?"

"I'll be home by six."

"We'll be there. We'll bring Chinese."

Laura smiled as she hung up. She was happy and her friend was happy. What could be better than that? And tomorrow she'd tell her all about Tal.

Promptly at six the next evening the doorbell rang. Laura opened it and hugged her friend, who then gleefully danced into the living room.

"Hi," Laura said to Yuusuf, standing in the hallway, his arms full of takeout bags from a local Chinese restaurant. "Come in. Congratulations to you both."

Yuusuf handed her the bags and Laura took them to the small dining table she had in an alcove of the apartment.

"Let me help," Jenna said, coming to the table. She flashed her left hand in front of Laura's face.

"Wow, what a rock!" Laura said. She dumped the bags and reached for her friend's hand, turning the finger slightly one way and the other to get the diamond to sparkle in the light. It was a marquise cut, large, and beautiful. It looked lovely on Jenna's hand.

Laura gave her another hug. "You'll have to tell me everything." She felt a small pang of envy, but pushed it away.

"Let's eat, I'm starved."

"Let me get the tea," Laura said, going into the kitchen.

"I thought people in love didn't have an appetite," Laura teased.

The phone rang when Laura was pouring the hot water over the tea.

"Can someone get that for me?" she called.

Yuusuf answered, waited a moment, then hung up. "No one there," he said.

The table had been set, the food ready for serving. Laura came in with the steaming teapot and placed it in the center.

Yuusuf seated Jenna, caressing her shoulders gently before he moved to his own chair.

Laura watched wistfully. She was happy for her friend, but she wanted the same kind of freedom to touch Tal, to laugh with things they'd done, to share family and friends.

"Guess what?" Jenna said, her eyes sparkling. "We're having an engagement part at Yuusuf's mother's estate in Tamarin. You have to come. Yuusuf will arrange everything. My folks will be there, some of our friends. But as maid of honor, you have to be at every party, I think there's some rule about that."

"I'd love to come if I can get the time off," Laura said. She'd always yearned to travel, how exciting to go to such an exotic setting as Tamarin, an Arabian country in North Africa—right on the edge of the Mediterranean Sea. "When?"

"In a week or two. It is important I take Jenna to meet my mother. I fear she will be more difficult to convince of our happiness than Jenna's parents. Once she meets her, however, how can she help but be captivated?" Yuusuf said.

Jenna raised her eyebrows in amusement and grinned at Laura. "I'm so charming, you know."

"It's not that," Yuusuf said.

She grew more serious. "No, it's the fact you keep hooking up with the wrong type of woman. Those days are over."

"Wrong woman?" Laura asked.

Yuusuf looked embarrassed. "There have been one or two, ah, incidents in my past in which I did not appear in the best light."

"Gold diggers out to nab him. He's too nice. He believed they loved him. Now he knows the difference," Jenna said firmly.

Laura nodded, not fully understanding.

"Imagine jetting to Tamarin, lying on the beach, soaking up the rays. Swimming in the warm water of the Med. I can't wait," Jenna said.

"And meeting my mother, my grandparents. There are more aunts and uncles and cousins on my father's side than you can imagine. I expect to have every moment we are there planned. I can only take a few days from work, so we'll leave on a Friday night, sleep on the plane and arrive in Tamarin Saturday afternoon. Coming back, however, we'll land only a few hours after we take off," Yuusuf said.

The discussion at dinner soon centered on the upcoming nuptials.

Tal stared out the window of his hotel room. The view of Union Square and the activity going on near the cable car turnaround had no appeal. Tourists crowded the streets and gave the scene a festive air.

His mood, however, was definitely not festive. Yuusuf had answered the phone when he called. Laura was still seeing him. Blast it. He thought she was beginning to see he would be a great catch, one who could offer her all her mercenary heart wanted. Yet she hadn't shifted her allegiance from Yuusuf to him.

What more would it take?

How far had Yuusuf gone in this infatuation? If he had proposed marriage, Tal would wring his neck. After the last woman had tried to get a commitment from his cousin, and Tal had bought her off, Yuusuf had sworn he would not fall for someone unsuitable. Until his love of the romantic overtook his good sense.

Tal was halfway tempted to go over to Laura's apartment and have it out with them both. How did she get away with spending both days of the weekend with him, and then turn around and see Yuusuf? What excuse had she given him about the weekend? Tal didn't see

Yuusuf patiently biding his time if he knew Laura was seeing someone else. Had he been away on business? Maybe she thought if he were gone, he'd never find out.

Tal turned from the window and strode to his laptop. His secretary had sent him reports which he should be reading. He disliked being so far from the office, and out of touch for so long, but this family matter was too important to ignore.

Especially since it seemed it was going to prove more difficult to woo the savvy Miss Toliver. He looked at the bracelet. He'd had the jeweler affix the new charm. The value had gone up considerably, of course, with the new diamond and sapphire gold charms. Maybe a more showy piece of jewelry was in order— a diamond or ruby necklace.

It appeared subtly was wasted on Laura. Tal didn't have all the time in the world. He wanted to get back to work. Waiting games had never suited him. And guessing what a woman thought was impossible. There had to be something he could do to hustle things along more quickly.

He'd force the issue next weekend. Surely Yuusuf wouldn't leave town twice in the same month on business. If Laura spent next weekend with him, his cousin would know it. Tal would make sure of it.

A cozy weekend for two. He smiled grimly. He knew it would cause problems all around when the deception was exposed. But by then, his cousin would be safe from another woman. In time, as with the other two cases, Yuusuf would come round. And be saved from the experience of Talique's marriage.

With patience hard won, Tal sat back down to review the work sent from his office. He would ask Laura to go away with him this weekend. Her answer would seal her fate.

CHAPTER SIX

LAURA had just brought a cup of coffee to her desk Tuesday morning when the phone rang. It was Tal. She glanced around, wishing she had a private office. No one seemed to be paying any attention, however, she could talk for a few moments.

"Hello. I didn't expect to hear from you today," she said. She was so glad he called. It made the endless wait until tomorrow night's dinner seem manageable.

"Just calling to confirm we are on for Wednesday night. What can I bring?" Tal said.

"Not a thing. I'll make a big pot of spaghetti and a salad and we can just relax in my apartment. It won't be too quiet an evening for you, will it?" Doubt began to creep in. Maybe Tal liked the glamour of nightspots, the fancy restaurants and the trapping of glittery nightclubs. Would he be bored to tears in her apartment and with the simple meal?

"I look forward to seeing you in your home setting. It establishes another layer for us to explore," he said.

"Layer?"

"In our relationship. I feel something special for you, Laura," Tal said.

Her smile felt as if it would split her face. She glanced around again. Still okay to talk.

"I feel something special for you as well," she replied, wishing she was confident enough to confess her love. Whether he ever came to care for her as much as she did for him, it didn't matter. Her feelings were not shallow or fleeting infatuation. She was old enough to know the difference even if she didn't have the experience.

"I was going to wait until tomorrow, but I'll ask now," he said.

She felt the breath go out of her. Was he going to ask her to marry him? Surely not over the phone!

"I have reservations for us at Lake Tahoe. Would you like to go this next weekend with me?"

"Go off for the weekend?" she said, surprised and excited. Another chance to be just the two of them.

"I have tickets for the show at the Romel Theater on Saturday night."

The Romel Theater was well-known for hosting spectacular events, from famous singers giving a full-blown concert, to world-famous circus acts, to plays from Broadway. She tried to remember if she knew what was currently playing. It didn't matter, any show they put on was fabulous.

"I'd love to go," she said, hoping she wasn't scheduled to work on the weekend. As far as she knew, Thursday and Friday evenings were taken up at the De Young Museum. After that, she was on her own until Monday.

"We could leave Friday night, come home Sunday," he suggested.

"I can't get away until Saturday."

"Ah. Well, then we'll leave Saturday, early."

"I might nap in the car," she said with a small laugh. "I'll be up late Friday."

"You may rest your head on my shoulder."

A flutter of excitement coursed through her.

"We can discuss it further at dinner tomorrow," she said, pleased to have future plans already made. It took away some of the uncertainty that she'd wake up one day never to hear from him again.

"Until tomorrow," Tal said.

"Oh, wow," Laura said softly as she hung up. She quickly dialed Jenna's number.

"You'll never guess where I'm going this weekend," she said as soon as her friend answered.

"And good morning to you, too. I didn't know you were going anywhere," Jenna said.

"Tahoe, and to the Romel Theater!"

"Oooo, so who's the rich guy taking you there. Those tickets cost the earth."

"Tal."

Jenna was quiet for a moment. "The new guy you're dating. What kind of name is Tal?"

"I think it's a nickname or something. Anyway, we spent most of this past weekend together and now he's invited me to go off this coming weekend. Jenna, I think I'm in love."

"You're kidding! Wait, are you at work? You waited until you were at work to tell me this? I need details and

I know you won't take long enough to tell me now. How could you wait so long? Why am I the last to know? I can't believe this!"

"Well, we were talking about your upcoming wedding last night, somehow the evening got away from us and I never brought it up. Besides, I'm sure Yuusuf wouldn't be the slightest bit interested in my love life."

"You better tell me everything from the beginning. Next time barge in with your own exciting news if I take over."

"You weren't taking over. And your news is more concrete than my fledgling feelings. Sometimes I'm so happy I can't stand it. Then I have a panic attack—what if I never see him again? I feel like a gawky schoolgirl one moment and then he says something or looks at me in the particular way he has and I feel like the most special woman on the planet. I can't talk now, I have to go, but I couldn't keep quiet about our trip. I'm so excited."

"Okay, lunch at one at that little place we like on Market. Be there!"

Laura laughed and agreed. Jenna wasn't the only one in love and excited about the future.

The restaurant was crowded when Laura entered. Jenna had arrived earlier and saved them a table near the back. With all the conversations going on, no one would pay the slightest attention to them. It was as private as it was going to get, Laura thought ruefully.

"I ordered shrimp salads. This place is a madhouse," Jenna greeted her.

"Thanks. Tourists combined with the usual workday crowd, I expect," Laura replied, slipping into her seat.

"So Tal is the man of the hour?" Jenna said.

"Maybe the man of my life. I'm in love," Laura said.

"For true? You're never in love. You like guys, date when it suits you. But in all the years I've known you, you've never been over the moon for anyone."

"I thought I was going to be left behind in the love stakes. Now I'm here to tell you that's not so."

Jenna reached over to hug her friend. "I'm so happy for you. When do I get to meet him. What's he like? I can't believe that you've fallen in love with some guy I've never met! But the timing is perfect. I found my Mr. Right, now you have, too. Best friends in everything."

"I think he's my Mr. Right. He's tall and dark and handsome. Is that such a cliché or what? But true. He's English, lives in London and works for a cruise line. And he's so romantic. We met at the McNab reception I worked. Then he found out where I worked, sent me flowers. Long stemmed pink roses. Their scent was heavenly."

"Forget the flowers, except that he gets good marks for the gesture. What's he like? Not just what he looks like. He has to be special to have attracted you."

Laura thought for a moment, trying to find a way to describe Tal in a few words.

"This is not a trick question, just tell me what you like about him," Jenna said impatiently.

The waitress wove her way through the crowd and set two brimming bowls of shrimp salad down in front of them. "I'll be right back with the beverages," she said, taking off.

"He's fun to be with. One night we went to dinner and dancing. Imagine a guy who loves to dance, and does so divinely. I felt like Cinderella at the ball. Saturday we went hot-air ballooning. Then Sunday he took me sailing. We had a picnic in a secluded cove up the coast a bit."

"Extravagant. Is that it?"

"I've only known him a short time," Laura said, taking her first bite.

"Love at first sight?"

"Yes."

"Laura, I've been in and out of love a dozen times since high school. When I met Yuusuf I knew the difference. But you're a babe in the woods. It could be infatuation."

"It could be, but I don't think so. He's not perfect," Laura said slowly. She liked these feelings. She didn't want Jenna to dim her happiness.

"How so?"

Laura thought a minute. "He's reticent. I have to pry information from him. And he's a bit more extravagant than I'm comfortable with, always bringing me presents, talking about his money, taking me to expensive places. Maybe he's trying to make me like him. Which he doesn't have to give me things to do. I can see myself married, with a bunch of children, all looking like him. And then growing old and still feeling this fluttering feeling when I look at him."

"Oh boy," Jenna said, ignoring her salad. "Are you seeing yourself old and gray around here?"

"He's from England."

"I heard that. So you'd have to move there?"

"He's never even hinted he feels the same about me, not in words. But he's so attentive I'm hoping he does, or will. Who knows what the future will hold," she said. She only knew what she *hoped* it would hold.

"At least that country speaks English. Tamarin's primary language is Arabic. I'm hoping Yuusuf will be able to continue working here. I can't imagine living in a country where I don't speak the language. But I have a hard time imagining my best friend living six thousand miles away."

Laura shrugged. "It probably won't lead anywhere." For a moment a great sadness welled. Was she setting herself up for a fall? Even now she felt her life would be less fulfilling without Tal in it. She felt as if a great weight descended on her shoulders. "There's nothing saying he feels the same about me."

"How could he not? I don't think true love is a one-way street," Jenna said.

"Oh come on, how many tales of unrequited love have we heard? It happens all the time."

"No, I think that's infatuation or something. Not true love. So when do I get to meet this wonderful man?"

"I don't know. He's coming to dinner tomorrow night, want to stop by?" Laura asked.

"I can't, I'm already committed somewhere. How about later in the week?"

"I'm working Thursday and Friday and then we're heading for Lake Tahoe early Saturday. We'll be home Sunday night. But I'm not sure what time. Maybe we can arrange to have dinner one night next week. I want you to meet him, and like him as much as I do."

"Call me Sunday night to let me know if you and he are still an item. No sense wasting my time meeting him if the weekend is a bust," Jenna teased. "You still haven't told me much about him."

Laura didn't know as much about Tal as she thought, she realized as she tried to explain him to Jenna. "I guess he went to some school in London, we haven't exchanged childhood stories yet. He mentioned Eton once."

The more she thought about it, the more she realized how very reticent Tal had been. Now that she thought about it, most of their talk had been of the newly met stranger variety. Or the questions he asked about her. She'd been so flattered he'd wanted to know all about her. How could she fall in love with a man she didn't know?

The thought worried her throughout the afternoon. At their next meeting, she'd make an effort to learn more about Tal, his thoughts, background and beliefs and values. Maybe it was time to be a bit more forthcoming with him. If he just wanted someone to casually date, she had better cut it off before she became so involved she'd be left with a lifetime of hurt.

Wednesday, Laura left work early to buy the ingredients for dinner. She splurged on a triple chocolate mousse cake from her favorite bakery for dessert. Spaghetti wasn't the most elaborate meal she could prepare, but she wanted to spend time with Tal, not be tied to the kitchen. Besides, she was only an adequate cook. He might as well learn that early.

Tal arrived promptly at seven. Greeting her formally, he handed her a large bouquet of spring flowers, daisies, tiger lilies, baby's breath and carnations. The colors of pinks and blues and whites were fresh and the mix charming. The sparkling crystal vase completed the arrangement.

"Thank you, they are lovely!" she said. "But you don't have to bring me something every time I see you."

He closed the door behind him and followed her into the living room. Laura set the bouquet on the coffee table, taking a whiff of the scented blossoms.

Tal withdrew the bracelet from his pocket and dangled it from his forefinger. "I had the jeweler put on the charms. We'll have to see if we can find one that looks like Lake Tahoe. If not, I can have one commissioned."

She took the bracelet and shook her head. "I don't need any more charms. These are special for our first days together." She held out her wrist. "Can you put it on me?"

He did, kissing her wrist when he finished, then tugging her closer until he kissed her mouth.

"I've missed you," he said. His dark eyes glittered with emotion. His face was so close to hers, she smiled and leaned closer to kiss him again.

"I've missed you, too," she said.

"What have you been doing since I saw you last?" he asked, straightening, and shrugging out of his suit jacket. He tossed it across the back of the sofa and began to roll up his shirtsleeves.

"Come in the kitchen to keep me company. Dinner's

almost ready. We'll eat at the table by the window. I've been doing routine background checks these last three days, in preparation for a large party next week. Oh, I do have news. My best friend got engaged over the weekend. I was asked to be in the wedding party."

When he stepped into the small kitchen, Laura was struck by how right he looked in the small room. If they were a couple, they'd spend a lot of evenings cooking together, talking about their time away from each other. Glad to be cocooned in the quiet of their own apartment.

"Can I help?" he asked.

"If you'd get the bread from the oven, I'd appreciate it. It's hot." She put the drained spaghetti into the large bowl and ladled sauce on top. The salad she took from the refrigerator and carried to the table. Wine was already opened on the table, the tall glasses at the tip of each knife.

The evening passed too quickly.

Sitting on the sofa together after dessert, Tal reached for her hand, holding it, gently rubbing his thumb across the back as he leaned back against the cushions to relax. Laura felt the thrill of anticipation to her toes. Sometimes she had trouble following the trend of the conversation so caught up was she with the awareness that threatened to overwhelm.

"You're working tomorrow night?" Tal asked.

"Right, at the De Young, the new Egyptian exhibit. And Friday night. But I'll be ready bright and early Saturday for our trip to Lake Tahoe."

"I'll pick you up at nine. We'll get there around lunchtime, explore a bit before dinner. I thought an early meal before the theater, then a late supper when the show is over."

"Sounds wonderful. Lake Tahoe's so pristine and beautiful. Have you been there before?"

"No. This will be another first for me."

She smiled, thinking he was alluding to more than a visit to Lake Tahoe. At least she hoped he was.

He kissed her as he was leaving. Long, slow, wonderful kisses. Laura hated to shut the door behind him. Why hadn't he kissed her earlier? More than once she'd felt he was keeping a tight rein on his emotions. Did that mean he wanted more, but was holding off until they knew each other better?

Waltzing around the apartment, she began clearing the table, and ran water over the dishes. She was already counting the minutes until Saturday morning. She was floating on air, dreaming about Tal even when she was awake.

Saturday dawned foggy and cool. The weather changed gradually as they left the coast behind and the limo wound through the Sacramento Valley toward the Sierra Nevada mountains in which Lake Tahoe nestled. The ride was smooth and quiet. Except for the scenery whipping by, Laura could hardly tell they were moving.

"Tell me about your evenings," Tal invited.

"I love doing museum events. The people attending those events usually are fascinated with the items on display, whether paintings, sculptures, or artifacts from a bygone era. While always on alert, I never feel the stress of private jobs. There are too many other security features for crooks to even think about stealing any-thing—at least not with so many other people around."

"But private parties are different?" he asked.

"Sure. We don't know anyone any more than we do at the museum. But guests are in the host's home. They could be targeting the place for a future robbery, or casing the guests to see who was wearing the most jewelry. Once at a senator's event, a woman was robbed in the ladies' room. We caught the thief, a teenage girl who wanted money for drugs. She had wrangled a job as server. Clumsy, but it could have been a bad scene."

"Is your job dangerous?"

"No. Mostly surveillance and background checks."

"Ah."

It occurred to Laura that she *could* do a check on Tal, find out more about him through the normal channels they used when vetting new employees for clients, or guests of dubious reputation. Not that she *would* now. Trust was an important aspect of any relationship. How hurt he'd be if she displayed such a lack. She had no reason to think he was trying some scam on her. What did she have of any value? He'd never asked her many questions about her work, nor about any of the firm's clients.

"Do you ever wish you were a guest at those affairs instead of security?" he asked.

She nodded, smiling in delight. "I'd love to have some exotic designer clothes, be part of the in crowd, jetting off to Cancún tomorrow for a few days. Who wouldn't?"

"Next time I get an invitation, I'll take you with me. I'll buy you whatever designer dress you like," he said slowly.

Laura looked at him. "I don't need anyone buying me clothes. The ones I have are fine. But if you wanted to take me to some fancy party, I'll be happy to be your date."

Tal had been a guest at the McNab fund-raiser. He obviously knew the kinds of people she worked for. Wouldn't it be fun to go to one of those as a guest! Though she doubted she'd have anything to say beyond what she said when she was working. Their realms were too far apart for her to comfortably fit in.

The air in the Sierra was crystal clear. The temperature comfortable with a slight breeze fluttering as they reached their destination. The Peaks was an exclusive hotel right at the state line between California and Nevada. The quiet elegance was an unexpected delight to Laura when they entered the ornate lobby. She felt as if she'd stepped into Wonderland. An old world Wonderland with rich mahogany, gilded columns and ornate frescos on the ceiling.

In less than ten minutes they were registered and whisked up to the top floor in a large mirrored elevator.

"I took the liberty of reserving a suite, with rooms for both of us, and a connecting sitting room," Tal said as they followed the bellman down the hall.

The carpet was so thick, Laura longed to take off her shoes to let her feet sink into the luxury.

The suite overlooked the Lake. The wide, high windows framed the beauty of the alpine waters with the tall pines and firs that came right to the water's edge.

"Gorgeous," she breathed, as she walked to the windows. She could look at this view for hours.

"Why don't you freshen up, and we'll go for lunch, then walk around," Tal suggested.

"Perfect," she said.

It was prophetic for the entire weekend. The walk took them along the busy main street with hotels and shops catering to tourists. Turning toward the lake, they soon reached the sandy shore where families and couples relaxed in the sunshine. Children frolicked in the cold water, laughing and splashing. Mothers called warnings, and fathers dozed on chaise lounges.

Dressing for dinner later, Laura gave a brief thought to Tal's offer to buy her a designer gown. She hoped the black cocktail dress she'd brought would be suitable. It would be nice to have a designer creation, but she'd be too afraid of damaging it to comfortably wear it. What if someone spilled something on it, or she tore it?

The musical at the Romel Theater was fantastic. On their way out, Tal had bought her a CD of the show's recordings. She would always remember that night whenever she played it. Not that she needed any external stimulus to remember every second spent with Tal.

They'd had a late night supper and danced beneath the stars on the rooftop restaurant at a nearby hotel. Sleeping in late on Sunday morning, they'd then partaken of a delightful champagne buffet their hotel provided for guests.

"I could get used to this," she murmured as she sipped champagne at eleven o'clock. She felt pampered and cherished. No wonder rich people liked being wealthy. But it wasn't the money that made the day special—it was Tal and the way he made her feel.

"It's something we could share again and again," he said, raising his glass in her honor.

"I'd love to," she said. Of course, she'd love eating hamburgers at a fast food place with Tal. It was the man she loved, the place was irrelevant.

The drive home detoured through the Napa Valley. This time instead of going hot-air ballooning, Tal had the driver stop at one of the many wineries made famous by the excellent vintage from Napa Valley. They took a tour of the facility, learning the different steps in producing the various wines. Ended in the tasting room, Laura was delighted to try samples of different kinds of wines produced. Tal bought a bottle of two of the ones she liked best.

When they reached her apartment building, it was just after seven. Laura invited him up. "We can order something in for dinner, or I can make an omelet. Not as glamorous as our meal last night, but the best I can throw together on short notice."

"It will be delicious, I'm sure," he said. Giving the limo driver the rest of the night off, Tal went with her into the building.

Opening the door a few moments later, Laura was surprised to see her friend Jenna sitting on the sofa.

"Hey, I didn't know you were coming over," Laura said. She could introduce Tal to her friend tonight. Tal followed her into the room, stopping just inside the door.

"I wanted to hear all—" Jenna trailed off when she saw Tal. "Oops, maybe this wasn't such a good idea."

"It's a great idea. Tal, this is my best friend, Jenna Stanhope. Jenna, Tal."

Jenna rose and held out her hand. Just then Yuusuf came from the kitchen, two glasses of water in hand.

"Tal! What are you doing here?" he asked in surprise.

CHAPTER SEVEN

FOR a moment everyone froze. The tableau would have been the ideal setting for a drawing room farce, only the perplexed expressions on three of the faces didn't fit comedy.

"You know Tal?" Laura asked.

Jenna let her hand drop, looking from Yuusuf to Tal.

"He's my cousin. I didn't know you were in the States. Last I heard—" Yuusuf looked at Jenna then at Tal.

"You're here because of me, aren't you? Dammit, leave me alone. This time it's different."

"You said that in Los Angeles," Tal said evenly. He carefully set the two bottles of wine on the table near the door. "Grandfather sent me."

"What's different?" Laura asked. She turned to Tal. "You're Yuusuf's cousin? I thought you were from England."

"Oh God," Jenna said. She sat on the sofa, looking at Laura with concern.

"With a name like Talique bin Azoz bin Al-Rahman you thought he was British?" Yuusuf asked.

Laura felt the world tilt beneath her. She looked at

Tal. "You said your name was Smith. I thought Tal was a nickname."

He looked at Yuusuf. "Grandfather saw the pictures in the newspaper, sent to him by someone in the embassy in Los Angeles. He dispatched me yet again to get you out of trouble."

"I am not in trouble. What pictures?" Yuusuf asked, going to stand near the sofa. He handed Jenna a glass of water, put his on the table and glared at Tal. "I'm definitely not in need of any rescue."

"The pictures were of you and Laura at some fancy party. He did not want a repeat of the previous incidents," Tal said evenly.

"What incidents? What's going on?" Laura asked. Tal seemed to withdraw, to hold himself apart from the rest of them, grow more remote.

"Sit down, sweetie. I don't think this is going to be good," Jenna said, patting the sofa beside her.

"I've just spent the weekend at Lake Tahoe with Laura. Does that sound like she's in love with you?" Tal asked Yuusuf harshly.

Laura sank beside Jenna, a dark premonition building. She couldn't take her eyes away from Tal.

"I hope she's not, it would sure complicate things," Yuusuf said.

"What?" Tal looked nonplused for a moment.

"I'm engaged to Jenna. We're flying home next weekend so mother can meet her, but they've already spoken a couple of times this week on the phone. I don't know what pictures you're talking about, but I'm not seeing Laura. Never have been."

Tal looked at Jenna.

She nodded, raising her left hand. "The picture I think you mean was taken at a party we were all attending—Laura working, Yuusuf and me as guests. They were standing together when the photographer snapped the shot. Laura, you remember, we laughed about it when we saw the gossip beneath."

Laura nodded. It didn't seem funny at the moment. She felt sick.

Tal looked at the engagement ring. "You're the one Yuusuf is seeing? There was yet another picture in last Saturday's paper coupling Laura and Yuusuf. How do you figure into all this?"

Laura heard the incredulity in his tone. She bristled in defense of her friend. So what if Jenna was a few pounds overweight, she was a warm and loving person. She wore her glasses today, but when she wore her contacts, she was as pretty as a picture. And she and Yuusuf were in love. Which seemed to have something to do with Tal's being here. She'd always known he had used a false last name. It hadn't seem to matter before.

"So do I get an explanation or is this twenty questions?" Laura asked, looking from one man to the other.

Yuusuf shrugged. "I had the unfortunate luck to become entangled with a couple of women in the past who proved to want my money more than they wanted me. My grandfather has a strong sense of family responsibility, especially since my father died when I was young. He sent Tal to the rescue, to make sure I didn't fall into the clutches of money-grubbing gold diggers, right, Tal?"

"He would have been better off letting you make a fool of yourself and learn a valuable lesson in the meantime," Tal said.

"But he didn't and you didn't. What was your plan this time? Drag me home. No, wait." Yuusef looked at Laura, then back at his cousin. "You're trying to make Laura fall for you and your fabulous wealth to demonstrate she only wants money. That's not like you, Tal. You should have just tried to buy her off like you did the others."

Laura felt as if Yuusef had kicked her in the stomach. She looked at Tal, waiting for him to hotly deny the charge. He said nothing, looking at his cousin without a trace of expression on his face.

"No," she whispered. Jenna reached out and grabbed her hand, squeezing tightly.

"So our relationship was a sham?" she asked.

"Relationship?" Tal responded. "Hardly that. I invited you out, you came. A casual date or two, does not comprise a relationship." But as he said the words guilt slammed through him.

Laura wanted to scream. Casual date or two? She'd pinned her dreams on a man who was trying to lure a fortune-hunting woman away from his cousin. Only he'd picked the wrong woman. She felt a sharp pain in the region of her heart. Then numbness began to spread.

"The presents and all?" Had they meant nothing?

"Most women like trinkets."

"This is the guy you were telling me about, Jenna?"

Yuusuf asked. "The one Laura—" He stopped. "Tal, you've gone too far this time. Both you and my grandfather can stay out of my life from now on. I think you should leave."

Tal felt as if he were in a world gone crazy. He'd been startled to find his cousin at Laura's apartment when they arrived. Initially he'd felt it the best thing—to have Yuusuf see his girlfriend returning from a weekend away with another man.

Only the scenario hadn't played out as he'd imagined. He looked at the slightly plump woman sitting beside Laura. She was close to Yuusuf in age, nice enough looking, but nothing like the beauties he normally squired around. Complacent and comfortable were descriptions that came to mind. And his cousin had asked her to marry him!

"There's still the matter of being wanted for your money," Tal said. He needed to get through to his cousin. His grandfather was depending on him not to allow Yuusuf to make a mistake. Tal himself didn't want his cousin to become disillusioned as he had been upon marriage.

"Jenna's family has had money since the California gold rush. Her father is a software engineer from the early dot.com days. He probably could buy and sell me, Tal," Yuusuf said. "I'm the one who has to fear they think I'm marrying her for her money, not the other way around. Though I hope after the grilling her father gave me last weekend, he knows I love Jenna. I want nothing from her but herself."

Stunned with Yuusuf's statement, Tal looked again at

the woman. She was not after his cousin for his money. They'd already talked to Yuusuf's mother and were planning a visit. Yuusuf had obviously met Jenna's parents.

Finally Tal looked at Laura. She was staring at the far wall. The painful expression on her face tore at his heart. She wasn't the woman he'd expected. The startling thought came that her feelings had genuinely been engaged. That she'd truly thought he wanted her.

"Laura."

"Please leave," she said between stiff lips. "I don't think we have anything further to say to each other."

"I'd like to explain."

"I think I get it. Just go!"

Tal looked at the other two, glaring at him in anger. The silence was deafening. With a brief inclination of his head, he turned and left the apartment.

He would carry Laura's face in his mind for a long time. He hadn't meant to hurt her. He'd enjoyed her company, though he never let himself forget she was after his cousin's wealth. Only, it looked as if he'd been completely wrong.

For a moment as he waited for the elevator, he considered the fact Laura wasn't involved with Yuusuf. She was free, perhaps they had started something they could salvage. Any relationship they had forged would not bring a rift to his family. If anything, it would solidify it with her being friends with Yuusuf's future wife.

He started to turn to talk to her to see where things might lead without the secrets between them. Hesitating, he shook his head. He'd wait until after Yuusuf and Jenna left. What he had to say was private for Laura alone.

As soon as the door closed behind Tal, Laura burst into tears. Jenna drew her against her shoulder.

"I'm so sorry, sweetie. I had no idea that your new man wasn't on the up-and-up. We came by today to hear about your weekend. I'm so sorry."

"You never mentioned his name, Jen. I would have guessed who he was, if you had," Yuusuf said. "Excuse me, I'm calling my grandfather." He went to Laura's phone and began to punch in the numbers.

Laura hardly noticed. Humiliation and pain burned through her. She felt as if she couldn't breathe. The ache in her chest was so sharp she was afraid she was having an heart attack. Tears wouldn't help yet she cried as she hadn't cried since her grandparents died.

"I thought he was wonderful and he was only making a play for me to lure me away from Yuusuf," she cried, as if saying the words would help her to understand them better. "Every single thing he did was orchestrated to have me fall in love with him just so he could walk away."

"It was cruel and unforgivable," Jenna said.

Sitting up, Laura yanked at the charm bracelet on her wrist. "Take it off!"

Jenna unfastened it and handed it to Laura. She threw it against the far wall. "Mementos to remember our time together. Ha, some memento."

She eyed the flowers.

"Don't. That's a Waterford vase, worth a small fortune. Even if you don't want it, don't smash it," Jenna said.

"Ohhhh." Laura's tears dried up. Anger replaced the hurt. "All I wanted was someone to love. Someone who wanted me for who I am. He thought I was a gold digger. He never even gave me a chance. I hate him." She jumped up and paced to the window, back to the sofa. "I wish I could pay him back. How dare he think I was after Yuusuf's money!"

"It's not too uncommon. Look at how protective my dad was about me," Jenna said.

"You're not taking his side?" Laura asked, horrified.

"Of course not. I'm not feeling a bit kindly toward him."

Yuusuf was talking in the background, in a language neither Laura nor Jenna understood. The tone of his voice was clear—anger flew across the wires. Whatever was said to his grandfather, had no effect in calming Yuusuf. He was still angry when he hung up the phone.

"Laura, on behalf of my family, I apologize. The actions of my cousin and grandfather are inexcusable. I only hope you realize I didn't know, or I would have stopped it."

"Of course I know you had no part of this. You're much too nice." Like she had thought Tal. Tears threatened again.

"Loyalty and concern, however misguided, were the driving forces in both Tal's and my grandfather's actions. Tal hates getting involved in personal matters. He'd much rather run his business and avoid all social contacts. Yet, family ties and loyalties are strong. It was for me," Yuusef said earnestly.

"He must have known Laura was falling for him. Look at all he did, presents, flowers, fancy dinners, elaborate dates and a weekend at Tahoe. It looks like a courtship to me," Jenna said. "No wonder Laura thought so as well."

Laura felt vindicated that she wasn't the only one to see it that way. It made her seem a bit less foolish.

Jenna rose. "Do you want us to stay?"

Laura shook her head. "Thanks for being here. I can't believe I was so gullible. If he hadn't been exposed tonight, who knows how long I would have blithely gone on." For a split second Laura wondered if it could have gone on forever, then reality surged back.

"Are you going to be all right?"

Laura nodded.

Jenna gave her a hug. "I'll call you later."

Laura nodded again, afraid to trust her voice. The anger was fading. The pain of Tal's betrayal taking hold again.

As soon as Jenna and Yuusuf left, Laura stumbled to her bedroom, flinging herself on the bed, facedown, and crying for all she had lost. She couldn't see how she would have known, but somehow, she should have known the lack of truth from Tal. Felt that he was only buying her, and biding his time.

It was after nine when the phone rang. Laura was lying on her bed, shoes kicked off, but unchanged from when she'd thrown herself down on the mattress earlier. She debated answering, but knew Jenna would get worried if she didn't. Rising, she went to the living room and picked up.

"Hi," she said.

"Laura."

She recognized the voice. "I have nothing to say to you," she told Tal, and hung up the phone. Glaring at it, anger grew. How dare he contact her after what he'd done. She went into the kitchen to prepare a cup of tea. She'd drink it, then get ready for bed. Despite all the drama in her life, she had to go to work in the morning.

The phone rang again.

She debated answering, then decided against it. She'd call Jenna once the phone stopped ringing, but she wasn't taking the chance of hearing Tal's voice again. Tears filled her eyes. She'd loved hearing his voice with its slight British intonation. She couldn't believe she was never going to listen to him again.

After about a dozen rings, the phone went quiet.

She lifted the receiver and dialed her friend.

"Did you just call me?"

"No. Yuusuf's still here. I was going to call later."

"I'm getting ready to go to bed."

"Are you doing all right?" Jenna asked.

"I will be. I'll call you in a day or two."

"Make it tomorrow," Jenna said.

Laura agreed then hung up. She unplugged the phone. Hoping Tal got the message, she was taking no chances of being disturbed again tonight.

Tal hung up, frustrated. She wasn't answering the phone, that much was clear. He'd tried a half dozen times. Leaning back in his chair, he stared out into the dark sky. Tal was confused. He knew something sparked between them. But a relationship?

Except, if she truly wasn't after a man's money, she might have seen it that way.

What a mess. He needed to explain, tell her he hadn't meant to hurt her, that he was looking out for his family. Women were big on family ties. Surely she'd understand.

The phone rang. Tal reached for it, surprised at the hope that bloomed. Maybe she'd relent and call him to hear his side.

"Tal, what have you done? Yuusuf called me earlier ranting and raving about interfering in his life and ruining a young woman of whom his fiancée is fond. Why is this the first I've heard of a fiancée? What happened to your grandiose plan to save your cousin from hurt and scandal?" It was his grandfather in full angry mode.

"It turns out Yuusef has found a woman I think will suit him. He's bringing her home soon to meet his mother," Tal responded. He wished he had taken more time before meeting Laura to learn the ins and outs of the situation. He and his grandfather had relied on the overzealous actions of an embassy employee. And Tal had been driven by love—not business. That had been his downfall. Hindsight was so good.

"So I found out when I talked to Yvette this morning. She likes her, but anyone can fool a person over the phone. We will see what she's like when she arrives."

"You will be surprised."

"And the woman you ruined?"

"Hardly that. The woman in the pictures we saw was not the one interested in Yuusuf." *She was interested in me,* Tal wanted to say, realizing with dismay how easily hearts could be broken.

"Do you like the woman he has chosen?"

"I hardly know her. But I believe Yuusuf is totally committed to her. She is unlike anyone else I've seen him with. And her family comes from money, so rid yourself of that worry."

"Hmmm. I will reserve judgment until I meet her. So your work is finished. Will you be heading for Bremerhaven next or returning home?"

"I'm staying another day or two." He made his mind up on the moment. He needed to see Laura again.

"Ah, to get acquainted with the new fiancée. Good idea. Call me after you talk with her."

Tal agreed, then hung up. He would get to know Jenna Stanhope. And learn what she could tell him about Laura.

Tal did not sleep well. He rose early and after using the fitness center at the hotel, showered and ordered breakfast. The pile of work awaiting his attention had not diminished over the weekend.

The knock at the door heralded breakfast. He opened it, only to find a bellman with a box. "Delivery for you," he said, holding it out. Tal took it, feeling something slide when the box tipped.

Putting it on the table, he opened it. The vase was inside, the flowers scattered around the box. In the midst was the bracelet with its sparkling charms and the CD. Everything he'd bought Laura had been promptly returned. He noticed an envelope. Opening it, several twenty-dollar bills fluttered out. She'd even calculated the cost of their dates and returned her share.

Anger flared. How dare she throw it all back!

Yet, what would he expect? He'd lied to her, accused her of being a gold digger. This was her way to repudiate the charge. Effective. And hurtful. Was this how she felt? He needed to explain to her. Make her understand why he'd done it.

Laura went to Jenna's after work. She didn't want to be alone. She'd spent most of the day working hard enough to keep thoughts of Tal at bay. But the evening would be endless if she were alone.

Jenna greeted her warmly.

"Yuusuf not here?"

"We're not married yet," Jenna said. "He's at the office still. I do hope he comes home at a reasonable hour when we are married. He says he has a lot to clear away before we fly to Tamarin. We're planning to leave next Saturday, arriving on Sunday. We've booked the flights. You did ask for time off, didn't you?"

"I don't think I'll go. This isn't the wedding. You don't need me for this visit." The last thing Laura wanted was to run into Tal again.

Jenna frowned. "If you don't go, neither will I."

"Don't be silly. You have to meet his mother and the rest of the family." Had things been different, Laura had once innocently thought she might have been the one going to meet Tal's parents. The ache in her heart was never far away.

"Tal will not be there. I'll make sure of that. I need

you to be with me, to shore me up. My parents aren't going until just before the engagement announcement. I'll be all alone."

"You'll have Yuusuf."

"I'll still be the outsider. Even once we're married, I'll be a stranger to the family for a long time. We don't share the same background, same language or customs."

"Are you sure about this marriage?" Laura asked.

"Oh, yes. I love him so much I ache with it. We were discussing where to live. Maybe a few months in the States and a few months in Tamarin each year. I don't know if I could go so far away from my parents forever. Or my best friend. Especially when the babies come. Who would be his favorite auntie otherwise?"

Laura tried to smile at her friend's passionate declaration. Two days ago she would have said the same thing about Tal. She'd loved him so much. Now she felt permanently damaged, as if there was an open wound that would never heal.

"You'll do fine. He'll make sure you don't feel like a stranger."

"I'm serious. Either you come with me, or I'll stay here. Yuusuf can send for his mother if she has to meet me right away."

"Oh, that'll be great for family harmony."

"It all rests with you."

"I don't like feeling pressured," Laura said.

"But I want you there. Please, for me, come with us."

Laura really didn't want to go. But Jenna rarely asked anything of their friendship. "Tal won't be there?"

"I'll get Yuusuf to make sure."

"Okay, I'll ask for time off tomorrow. But if my boss says no—"

"If he says no for this next week, find out when it will be okay to take a week or so off and we'll go then."

Laura wanted her friend to have the best wedding ever. If her going to Tamarin with Jenna assured that, she'd do it. Her friend would probably be marrying for the both of them. Laura didn't see herself finding another man to love as she had loved Tal. Once burned, twice shy was the old saying. And she'd turned twenty-eight before she had fallen in love for the first time. How long would it take to forget the man who had taken her heart and so ruthlessly rejected it, all in the name of family?

CHAPTER EIGHT

THE flight from San Francisco to London, and then on to Tamarin took more than eighteen hours. Despite the luxury of first class all the way, Laura was exhausted by the time they landed in the desert country of Yuusuf's birth. She hoped they could quickly meet his mother and then she could be excused to catch up on sleep.

Her fatigue was undoubtedly made worse by the fact she hadn't been sleeping well at night for more than a week. Tossing and turning, she rarely slept five hours all told. And that was often disturbed by nightmares. She worked hard during the day, to keep unruly thoughts at bay.

"It's beautiful," Laura said when they walked out of the airport into the sunshine. The humidity was higher, the temperature warmer than in San Francisco, making the air seemed close and thick.

The scent of flowers filled her senses. Laura felt her heart lift a fraction. The tall palm trees and banks of colorful fragrant flowers gave the airport a friendly feeling missing in the glass and concrete airport of San Francisco. Maybe being here would help ease the pain of the past few days. There was so much to see, new people to meet, things to do. With Tal absent, she would force herself to enjoy every new experience.

A white limousine slid to a quiet stop. The driver came round to open the door and take care of the luggage. For a moment, Laura's heart skipped a beat. It was not the same vehicle from California. She took a deep breath and climbed inside, sitting in the seat opposite Jenna and Yuusuf.

"We'll drive straight to my mother's villa," Yuusuf said. "That's where we're staying. I know you both are tired. After a nap, we'll meet my mother's immediate family at supper."

"Which will be your mother, your aunt Sophia and your grandparents Camille and Anton, right? Goodness, will I ever keep them all straight?" Jenna asked.

"You'll do fine. My mother is Yvette. Aunt Sophia's name you know. Her husband is Aziz bin Tammur. He's a doctor. My grandparents will love you. Anton and Camille. They're French, as I told you. My father's father is the one who sent Tal. He and grandmother Abree will come tomorrow. I'm still angry about the situation. Especially for you, Laura," Yuusuf said.

"I'm fine. I look forward to meeting your mother. And seeing your home here in Tamarin." Did Tal have a house or a flat? Did he spend a lot of time here, or more time in London? She wondered, but dare not ask. She felt a slight pang, knowing it no longer mattered.

The drive through the city went quickly. The tall skyscrapers of glass and steel reflected each other in the ubiquitous mirrored windows used to keep the heating load manageable.

Parks and wide flower-lined boulevards made the city truly lovely. Laura was interested to see all the people in western attire. She'd thought she'd see the long robes and veils usually associated with Arab countries. Occasionally she did see a couple dressed in more traditional attire, but they were few and far between. She could have been in Paris or Rome.

The cars zipping along showed traffic was a problem everywhere.

Soon they reached a residential section with homes built on one or two acres of land, beautifully landscaped. Of the houses she could glimpse from the road, white was the predominant color, with bright tiled roofs. When the limo slowed to turn into a long driveway, she looked with interest at the home Yuusuf had grown up in. This would be her friend's new family. Laura hoped they all loved Jenna.

She had her doubts about the grandfather who had tried to prevent Yuusuf from getting involved. He she was not prepared to like.

Yvette bin Horah was a gracious hostess. She embraced Jenna and her son and offered a warm welcome to Laura. She had tea and small sandwiches ready and urged them to refresh themselves.

"You all must be so tired after such a long flight. I do not like that mode of transportation. I have arranged supper to be a little late, at eight. As soon as you've eaten, I will show you to your rooms. Do rest up."

The villa was all on one floor, with hallways going

off in different directions. Yvette led the way to a wing off the main salon and opened the first door for Laura. "This is for you, my dear. I do hope you'll be happy. It opens off onto the gardens."

"It's lovely."

Laura stepped inside and was instantly enchanted. The room was bright and washed in yellow from the pale walls to the bright coverlet on the bed. White curtains blew in the breeze coming in through the French doors that led to the garden.

"You must be an excellent gardener. I've never seen such gorgeous flowers before," she said, walking to the French doors. Despite the beauty, the bed beckoned.

"Rest. We'll see you at dinner." Yvette closed the door softly.

Laura's suitcase sat near the closet. She lifted it and found it empty. Someone had already unpacked. She opened a drawer and found a nightie. Donning it, she gratefully slid beneath the cool sheets on the bed. It was heavenly. Far from San Francisco, far from Tal and the debacle of their brief time together, Laura felt herself relax. Soon she slipped into welcomed sleep.

Laura was treated as an honored guest. At dinner she met Yuusuf's mother's family—her sister Sophia, and her parents Anton and Camille. The conversation was vivacious and centered around the coming wedding.

Laura was included in all the planning stages, listened to when occasionally she had a comment to make. She tried to enjoy the happiness of her friend. Only once during the evening did she think she had recently hoped to have a similar event in her own life.

Fairy tales didn't come true. She banished Tal from her thoughts and focused on the suggestions Aunt Sophia continued to make. If the woman had her way in everything, Jenna's wedding would be an extravaganza not long forgotten.

The next day Yuusuf took Jenna on a drive. Laura took advantage of the free morning to enjoy the gardens. She ran into Yvette around eleven o'clock and the two sat together in an arbor sheltered from the hot sun by a trellis thick with grape leaves providing shade. A sparkling fountain gurgled nearby.

"I am happy for my son," Yvette said. "The woman he chose this time is perfect for him."

"I take it there were a couple of other times when the woman wasn't so perfect," Laura said neutrally.

"Oh, the woman in Boston was the worst. She would have married him and made his life hell. She was bought off by his grandfather. I never knew how much he paid, but I have always thought it a small fortune. Tal handled that for Salilk, of course. Salilk had just had bypass surgery and wasn't well. And he was definitely not happy with Yuusuf at the time."

"Sounds like a narrow escape for Yuusuf." Her view of Jenna's intended changed slightly.

"My son was young. Sheltered. He wanted to go to America where we do not have a large circle of friends, so he was on his own. Flattery will go so far in turning a young man's head, don't you think?"

She thought about her own feelings when Tal had sought her out, made her feel as if she were the only woman in the world. Flattery had certainly turned her head. She hated thinking how easily she'd fallen into a similar trap.

"Yes, you are right."

"Yuusuf asked to work at the California office of the family shipping firm. He then fell in love with a movie starlet in Los Angeles. I think she hoped he'd buy a film company and give her the leading roles. Men can be so blind. Though I do think some of his stubbornness was in reaction to his grandfather's high-handed behavior in Boston."

Yvette leaned back and sighed. "It's so lovely here. I don't understand my son's love of living in America. We have all the modern conveniences you have in your country and more."

"Maybe it's a way to stay from under his grandfather's thumb," Laura replied dryly.

"Oh, Salilk just sends Tal. Tal loves his family and would do anything for Yuusuf. He is his favorite, you know."

"No, I didn't." It was obvious from the conversation that Yvette hadn't a clue what had transpired between Laura and Tal. And Laura didn't plan to enlighten her.

"Tell me what you do," Yvette said. "Always women work in America. Except Jenna. Though her volunteer duties could be considered work, I suppose."

"I'm employed by a security company," Laura said. She explained her duties, sharing some humorous anecdotes.

"I would have loved to have seen that," Yvette commented, laughing at one of her stories. "We would not have that here."

"But you have not always lived here," Laura said.

"True. My father was in the diplomatic corps. My sister Sophia and I had tutors in English, French and German. When my father was posted here, I also studied Arabic. Of course that was the right thing to do when I met Yuusuf's father. Laban was a wonderful man. I still miss him fiercely. We were only married seven years. I've been a widow for more than twenty-five years. Soon, I may be a grandmother. When I think of all he's missed, I feel so sad."

"I'm sorry to hear that," Laura said. She could almost relate. Tal had not died, but her love had. Would she mourn for twenty-five years? She hoped not!

"My mother said I would find someone else. But it hasn't happened. Sometimes I think a woman is meant for one special man."

Laura hoped she was wrong. She didn't want to miss Tal the rest of her life. She needed to focus on how betrayed she felt. Focus on his treachery not the romantic tones he'd set—which had proved to be so false.

"You never returned to France?" Laura asked gently.

"Oh, I go every year for a few weeks. But this is the home Laban made for me. Here I feel close to him. I will never leave."

Laura wondered if she should move from her apartment. Tal had only had one meal there, yet it seemed every place she looked reminded her of him.

"It just takes time," she murmured.

"What does?" Yvette asked.

"To get used to new things," Laura said.

* * *

By the time Tuesday afternoon arrived, Laura had worked herself up into a case of nerves. She had enjoyed meeting Yvette's parents, but she dreaded meeting Tal and Yuusuf's mutual grandfather.

She lay down for a short nap, but couldn't sleep. The house was quiet. Slipping out into the gardens, she wandered near the fountain with the sparkling spray. She loved the sound and the bright flowers that surrounded the stone base. She sat on one of the many benches that were scattered throughout.

"Yvette has the prettiest gardens in the area, I've always thought," a familiar voice broke into her reverie.

Laura rose abruptly and turned. Tal stood not ten feet from her.

"What are you doing here?" Laura couldn't help a spurt of excitement, which she quickly snuffed. He looked tired, as if had just arrived and suffered jet lag. She remembered their first conversation about travel at the McNab's affair.

"Invited by my grandfather to meet Yuusuf's bride. I'm surprised to find you here," he said.

Laura turned to leave, escape foremost in her mind. But he proved quicker, reaching her before she took three steps, taking her arm.

"Let me go," she said, struggling briefly to free herself. But his grip was firm.

"I want to explain."

"I know all I need to know from Yuusuf. We have nothing further to discuss."

"I think we do."

Laura glared at him. "Very well, say what you have to say so I never have to see you again."

He gave her a wry look. "Sounds like you're going to listen to me with an open mind."

She looked away, wishing she was strong enough to pull away and leave him behind. Part of her yearned for him to say some magic words that would wipe away the days of hurt and make things right. But she didn't see how that was possible, not given what she already knew.

She waited.

Tal was silent for a long moment. Did he plan to speak at all?

"Yuusuf is a wealthy young man, who had no sense of his self-preservation. Nor is he particularly sophisticated. About six years ago he fell into a situation in Boston—"

"I've heard about that. And the affair in Los Angeles. And how big, strong, *sophisticated* cousin Tal rode to the rescue. None of that has anything to do with me. You saw me as a threat to Yuusef and came in like a masked avenger. You should at least have gotten your facts right."

"Hardly masked."

"Smith isn't a form of hiding? Why not tell me your real name? Because you knew Yuusef would recognize it instantly if I mentioned it to Jenna. Heck, if you'd told me your true name the first thing I would have done was ask if you knew him."

"The fact of the matter is our grandfather is not in robust health. He worries about Yuusef. I am a dutiful grandson. I followed family tradition by going to school in England. Married the woman my parents picked for me."

Laura jerked around and stared at him. "You're married?" It made everything more despicable.

"Not anymore. She died. The point I'm trying to make is that to my grandfather, at least, I seem more settled, less likely to be taken in by a fortune hunter. But Yuusuf has already had two narrow escapes. We were trying to find a way to make him a bit more wary about women throwing themselves at him. It was not a good plan and I apologize for my part in it. I never meant to cause you harm."

"You just wanted to lure me away from the fortune you thought I was after by dangling an even bigger one and then dump me."

"I would have made it worth your while. The settlements on the other two were quite exorbitant."

"That's it? That's your explanation?" Laura was not appeased.

He nodded.

"Your original plan worked with the other two, why not stick with that? One offer of a huge check, which I would have told you to shove, and you'd have known I wasn't interested in Yuusuf. And you could have avoided all the nasty work of pretending to be interested in someone you obviously despised. And the costly presents you so generously tried to bribe me with."

"I don't despise you. Even when I thought you were after Yuusuf, I never felt that. You have fascinated me from the very beginning." His voice changed, became gentle, almost hypnotic. "I like the way you see things with such enthusiasm. Our balloon ride was special because of your delight. You're staunchly loyal to your friend. And you have integrity that many women your age do not possess. You are quite different from—well from women I've known."

"Like attracts like." Only in her case, it hadn't. Laura looked away, horrified to find tears threatened again.

"Come, let us make up. It will make things run more smoothly while you are visiting. Who knows, we might become friends again," Tal said.

She succeeded in pulling free. "I don't think we were ever friends, Tal. And I have no intention of taking up with you in any way, shape or form. I'll stay in my room while you're around. That will make things run as smoothly as you could wish." She spun around and almost ran back to her room, firmly closing the double French doors and latching them.

Her first instinct was to pack her bags and find a way home. But that would probably be impossible, not to mention rude. Still, Jenna had assured her Tal wouldn't be around, and yet here he was.

Damn him! How dare he try to gloss over the situation. She couldn't forget how he'd acted as if he really liked her. Taking her special places, pretending to be interested in all she had to say. It was all false. Honeyed words now couldn't change the past. Or mend a broken heart.

She'd plead a headache and stay in her room while the others dined tonight. By tomorrow Yuusuf's grandfather and cousin would be gone and it would be safe to venture forth once again.

Safe? Was she that afraid of her feelings for Tal?

A knock sounded on her door. If he had come

through the house to try to cajole her into doing what he wanted, she had words for him.

Flinging open the door, Laura was surprised to see Jenna there. Her friend stepped inside and shut the door.

"I'm so angry I could spit," Jenna said. She looked at Laura. "Tal is here. Yuusuf assured me he wouldn't come, but he just showed up. His grandfather apparently invited him. This isn't even his house. I'm not sure I'm looking forward to meeting *him*, either. How could they treat Yuusuf like he was a little boy or something."

"Not to mention the way they treated your best friend," Laura murmured.

"I don't need to mention that, because we've already been through it. I think I'll take a tray in here with you," Jenna said, flouncing over to the bed and sitting on the edge.

Laura smiled. "I have a headache. I was going to ask to be excused from dinner."

"Maybe it's contagious," Jenna said. She flopped back. "I can't believe the way things are turning out. We should have stayed in San Francisco."

"Why? I think Yvette is charming. She'll be such a wonderful mother-in-law. And I like her side of Yuusef's family. Don't you?"

"She is sweet, and I like her parents as well. But the machinations of the paternal side of Yuusuf's family are not what I'm used to. To have them act as if he doesn't know his own mind is infuriating."

"You need to go to dinner. This will be your family for the rest of your life. You need to start on good terms," Laura said practically.

"Not if you don't come."

"Not this time."

"So you let Tal win?" Jenna said.

"Win?"

"I say put on your best outfit, your sexiest makeup to show off your looks and face him at dinner as if nothing happened. In fact, ignore him. Don't give him the satisfaction of thinking he meant more to you than you meant to him." Jenna sat back, her eyes sparkling with excitement. "Show him what you're made of, girl."

"He had to know what I was feeling," Laura said doubtfully.

"Did you ever say anything specific—like I love you, Tal?"

"No."

"Then anything he suspects is just that, guesswork. Guys are dumb, he probably hadn't a clue. He was seeing you as some witch after his precious cousin. Come on, Laura, you can do it. Let's go united against the males in this family—except for Yuusuf of course."

"Of course." She considered it. Could she pull it off? She'd felt so humiliated knowing she'd been falling in love when all the while Tal had been deliberately enticing her only as an act. If he hadn't guessed how she had felt, no reason to give him that information now.

She owed it to herself, to her self-respect to show the world his actions had no lasting effects. She'd smile, be gracious to the other members of the family and totally ignore Tal and his grandfather. Laura thought about it long and hard.

"Okay. I do have the perfect dress, if you don't think

it'll be over the top. I brought it for the engagement party, but maybe I'll wear it tonight as well." It was one of her favorites, deep blue, it hugged her figure, and did wonderful things to her complexion. Not to mention her self-esteem.

Despite the pep talk, Laura's nerves were at the screaming stage when she walked down to the gathering later that evening. She knew she looked good, which was a help. But her emotions were too raw to feel complacent about the charade she was attempting. She had to greet Tal and his grandfather as if they were strangers in passing. How much of what had gone on did the others in Yuusuf's family know?

Head held high, Laura entered the drawing room. For an instant she felt the crowd already gathered was more than she could deal with. Then she saw Jenna standing to one side. For a moment she worried her friend had been shunted out of the mainstream, until she saw her smile at something said by a diminutive woman at her side.

Homing in on her like a beacon, Laura ignored the rest.

"Laura, come and meet Madame ibn Horah. She's Yuusuf's other grandmother, and a most delightful lady," Jenna said.

"How do you do?" Laura said. She'd already met Yvette's parents, so this was Tal's other grandmother. Married to the sheikh who tried hard to protect his younger grandson, no matter the cost.

"I'm happy to meet you," Madame ibn Horah said, holding out her hand. The jewelry on her fingers glittered in the light.

She was a petite woman, dressed in a gold gown which was very conservative in cut and style.

"Laura has been my best friend since we were little girls," Jenna said. "She met Tal in San Francisco. He thought she was me. Or rather, that she was the one Yuusuf was interested in."

Laura could have groaned aloud. If no one knew how she'd made a fool of herself over a man bent on proving she was a fortune hunter, she'd have liked to keep it that way.

"So you were the decoy while Yuusuf and Jenna had time to find out if they were really suited without stupid interference from the men in my family," Madame said, smiling. "A job well done."

Laura smiled politely. Now she was a decoy. At least it gave her a higher standing than dupe.

Tal had seen Laura enter the room a few moments ago and join Jenna and his grandmother. They seemed to be getting along well. He admired her for showing up. After fleeing from him in the garden, he wouldn't have been surprised if she'd pleaded a headache or something to avoid the gathering.

Heading in their direction, he arrived just as his grandmother complimented her on a job well done. What had she done?

"Good evening," he said.

Jenna looked at him with an expression of loathing. Laura turned, smiled politely and appeared to be looking over his left shoulder.

"Good evening," she said politely.

"Oh, do excuse us, Madame," Jenna said. "Laura, Aunt Sophia has just arrived and you know how much you wanted to see her. I'll make sure we have time to chat after dinner, Madame." Jenna swept by Tal without a word.

Laura quickly followed.

"That went well," he murmured, following Laura with his eyes.

"So, maybe the young lady didn't like being cast in a role not of her choosing," his grandmother said.

Tal looked at her. "They told you?"

"Your grandfather told me of your scheme to make some woman change her allegiance from Yuusuf to you. How could you ever hope to accomplish that without some emotional involvement? You two should have trusted Yuusuf. He's been very circumspect since the incident in Los Angeles. Why did you not give him the benefit of the doubt?"

"Grandfather was worried. I did it for him," Tal said, feeling like a small child being chastised by his grandmother.

"I've already had words with your grandfather. Tell me, what do you think of Jenna's friend?"

Tal looked across the room where Laura laughed at something Yuusuf's Aunt Sophia was saying. She looked heartbreakingly beautiful. He watched her for a long moment, wondering if she'd ever laugh again with him.

"I was wrong about her," he said slowly.

His grandmother was watching him speculatively. "I think she was very hurt," she said softly in their language.

"I did not mean to hurt her."

"Nonetheless. Now what do you plan?"

He smiled down at his grandmother. "That is not for discussion."

She nodded, smiling sweetly. "Your grandfather is sometimes narrow in his view of the world. Do not become like him."

"I won't."

"Yasmine has been dead for four years."

"I know that."

"It is time you thought about marriage again, Tal. Not every woman is as selfish and greedy as she." He said nothing. He should have known what Yasmine was like. The fault of his marriage lay with him. His emotions had been clouded by that.

"Maybe it's not only the men in this family who try to interfere," his grandmother said.

He hoped he could keep the past from influencing the decision he'd come to over the last few days. He wanted Laura. He hadn't realized how much until he'd seen the hurt and pain in her eyes that night Yuusuf revealed their connection. He'd made a colossal mistake, one he wasn't sure he could ever rectify. But he wouldn't quit until all hope of making amends had died.

"So, my boy, you are home safely," Salilk said, joining his wife and older grandson.

"As you see. I arrived last night. Are you sure it was wise to include me in this gathering? Yuusuf is angry, his bride-to-be borders on rudeness and the woman I mistakenly thought was after Yuusuf's money won't even look at me. Not a harmonious family evening," Tal said wryly.

"I have already spoken to the consulate in Los Angeles, telling them of the error and suggesting they investigate claims more thoroughly before passing them on to us. However, everyone appears cordial, that's a first step. Jenna is not what I expected."

"She's quite lovely," his wife said.

Salilk looked at her and frowned. "Do you think?"

"Inside, where it counts most. Do credit Yuusuf for picking a woman of character and strength to marry. I predict it will be a happy life for them both."

"Then I had better try to mend fences with my future cousin-in-law," Tal said. He knew time would eventually heal all wounds, but he didn't have a lot to spare if he was to get back into Laura's good graces before she returned to America. Even to himself, he wasn't entirely sure what he meant by that. He wanted her to laugh with him again. See the shining enthusiasm that she so readily displayed. Kiss her again. Have her look at him with that special light in her eye.

He headed across the room to where Jenna and Laura stood. No time like the present to start.

As if sensing his approach, Laura said something to Jenna and she and Sophia moved away. Jenna looked at Tal.

"I have apologized," he said when he drew near.

"That doesn't make it better," she said.

Yuusuf joined them immediately, as if defending his future bride from Tal.

"I asked my mother to exclude you from the guest list tonight," Yuusuf said, glaring at Tal.

"I know. I'm crashing on orders from grandfather."

Yuusuf drew in a breath. "If I could have excluded him, I would have done so as well."

"At least give us credit for having the right motives, even if the execution was clumsy," Tal said easily. He couldn't fault his cousin for his responses. He was beginning to understand how deeply he had offended Laura.

Given the true nature of the situation, he'd been insulting to all three. Yet, if Yuusuf had become involved again with another fortune hunter, the end result would have been vastly different. For a moment Tal regretted not being seen as the hero in all this. Instead he was the villain, a role he did not relish.

"I regret what happened," he said, his eyes searching for Laura. She and Sophia were not in sight. Maybe they were visiting the gardens before dinner.

"Please do me the courtesy of leaving immediately after dinner, and do not bother my mother's guests again while they are here," Yuusuf said stiffly.

Tal looked at him. His younger cousin had grown up. He stood eye to eye with Tal, and his voice was firm and sincere.

"As you wish. Even before, since I am not wanted. I do extend my sincere congratulations on your engagement. Your future bride is perfect." Tal inclined his head to both, and turned to leave.

He found Yvette and gave his regrets.

"You must stay, your leaving will throw off the seating," she said.

Pained that was the only reason she wanted him to remain, Tal remained firm. "I believe it best." He kissed her cheek gently. She'd always been a favorite of his. "I'm sorry for the upset."

"All's well that ends so happy for all of us," Yvette said.

If that were only true, Tal thought as he left the villa. Jenna and Yuusuf were happy, of that there was no doubt. But Laura? He'd seen the sadness lurking in her eyes. And he felt an inch tall knowing he'd put it there.

He'd insulted her, hurt her.

For a moment he stopped, thinking back to their time together. She'd been happy, he'd known that. He'd thought it because she was delighted with the expensive trinkets he gave her, or the lavish entertainment he planned.

But she'd been equally as happy the night they'd had dinner at her apartment. Maybe he hadn't only damaged her pride. Had he hurt her because of a growing affection? Or more?

CHAPTER NINE

LAURA made it through the dinner and retired as soon as she could without causing comment. Tal had left before the meal was served. She felt triumphant that her appearance had apparently caused him to leave. But there was a lingering sadness that he was no longer welcomed in his family's home. In the greater scheme of things, she'd be gone in another few days. Tal would be dealing with Yuusuf's family for the rest of his life.

As she would, when Jenna and Yuusuf were in America.

A compromise had to be reached.

But not on her end. It had taken all her strength and pride to keep from shouting at him, railing against him that he could have so carelessly toyed with her affections, knowing from the very beginning that there was no future for them.

The strain showed, she thought, looking into the mirror after getting ready for bed. Her eyes looked haunted. There were fine lines around them that used not to be there.

And her heart ached.

Turning off the lights, she wandered to the open French doors. The cool night breeze set the gauzy curtains billowing. The fragrances from the various blossoms filled the air, sweet and exotic. She leaned against the door, hearing the soft murmur of distant voices as the party continued.

The sound accentuated her loneliness. With her grandparents gone, she had no one left. Jenna was not only her best friend, she was her only old friend who had known her grandparents.

The hope for a bright future had been dashed. Tal had been like a fairy-tale prince, only he'd turned into a frog. She was still young, healthy and had a wide circle of friends. She would not allow recent events to sour her on life.

Tears threatened again. She swallowed hard. She was trying to be brave, but her heart broke. She'd been so happy thinking Tal had loved her. But she'd been fooling herself all along. The reality was more painful than she could deal with.

As she crawled between the cool sheets of her bed a short time later, she rather thought she would like to go through life never hearing Tal's name again.

Take one day at a time. It was all she could do.

The next afternoon Yuusuf took Jenna and Laura to the beach. Because it was a Wednesday afternoon, it was not crowded. Colorful umbrellas lined the edge of the water. Lounge chairs marched beneath them like a drill team. Laura smiled, thinking of taking a towel and lying on the sand the few times she went to the beach at home.

"Lovely," Jenna said. "And the water's warm!"

"Not like San Francisco, that's for sure," Laura agreed. They went for a swim, then Laura lay on one of the chaises beneath an umbrella near the water's edge while Yuusuf and Jenna went for a walk along the shore. The Mediterranean didn't have a surf, just gentle waves lapping the shore. She could feel herself grow drowsy. Maybe a nap wouldn't hurt.

"Enjoying the afternoon?"

She groaned, hoping she was imagining that voice. Risking it, she opened one eye, promptly closing it again.

"What are you doing here?" she asked Tal.

She heard the chair next to hers creak as he sat beside her. He wore shorts and a knit top. His arms were muscular and tanned.

"Wednesday is the afternoon I usually take off. Can't work all the time." He settled back in his chair, his gaze on the water.

Laura sat up and looked left and right. "There are about two hundred empty chairs on this beach," she said.

He nodded, not looking at her.

"Why sit on that one?" she persisted.

"It's convenient."

"How so?"

"It's next to yours."

"Then I'll leave it to you and find another one."

"I'll follow."

Laura stared at him, afraid she was going to laugh at the picture that popped into mind. Musical chairs on the beach. She jumping up and getting a new chair, he taking the one next to it. Her popping up again. With two hundred chairs, they could be at it all afternoon.

Sighing, she lay back and closed her eyes. She could ignore him. Yet there was a tingling awareness that defied ignoring. She felt his presence as if he touched her.

"Have you seen much of Tamarin?" he asked politely.

"Not much. What I've seen is pretty."

There was silence for a moment. Laura was beginning to relax, hoping he'd remain silent. She could almost imagine she was alone.

"I could show you around," Tal offered.

"I don't think so."

"Why not? Yuusuf is taken up with Jenna. I know from what Yvette said last night that he's planning to take her to visit some of his friends tomorrow. Of course, I'm sure you'd be included."

"Great, I'll be a spare part."

"Exactly. You don't have anything planned. Let me show you around."

"What is this, some kind of peace offering?"

"And if it were?"

Laura thought about it. She couldn't help but feel more alive. How dangerous would it be to let him show her around? She'd spend a few hours in his company. Sheesh, how pathetic was that? He'd been leading her on and now she wanted to spend more time in the man's company after what he'd done? She needed to keep her distance.

"Come on, Laura. Our seeing each other in San Francisco wasn't all about Yuusuf. We enjoyed being together. Admit it."

She rolled her head to her left and looked at him. "I did have fun. I thought it was real."

"The enjoyment was real. It was only the motivation behind the invitations that was not. I, also, enjoyed the times we spent together." His dark eyes caught hers, held.

She yearned to believe him. To hold on to the hope that everything he had said had not been calculated and false. Yet how would she ever separate truth from deliberate falsehood? How could she ever trust him again?

"One of our cruise ships will be docking tomorrow morning. I can take you aboard if you like, show you what one looks like."

Laura remembered he'd casually offered that in San Francisco. She knew he never expected to have to honor that offer. She'd love to see it. When else would she get a chance to see a ship. Yet, dare she risk being so long with Tal?

"Very well, I accept. But only to see the ship." The instant she accepted doubts arose. She still felt unsure of herself, embarrassed she'd fallen so fast for a man who was manipulating her.

If she hadn't been feeling a bit left out of the festivities for Jenna and Yuusuf, Laura would not have agreed.

"I have a view of the sea from my house," Tal said.

"Mmm." Instantly curious about his house, she wished he would describe it. She was not going to show interest. She was not going to be enticed into thinking there was anything more to his invitation than to keep harmony in his family.

"My gardens are not as lovely as Yvette's, however. Yasmine was the gardener, not me. I have a crew that comes in once a week."

"Was Yasmine your wife?"

"Yes." His voice was clipped.

Laura longed to learn more—had she been beautiful, accomplished? How had she died? What did he miss most about her? Was his heart buried with Yasmine? She'd bite off her tongue before indulging her curiosity.

When the silence stretched out several moments, Tal spoke. "Yasmine died of an aneurysm. One minute she was laughing at something, the next she screamed in pain and died."

"How awful. I'm so sorry. How long ago?"

"Four years. We'd been married for seven." Once again his voice sounded odd.

"You must still miss her."

"Not at all," he said cooly.

Her eyes opened and she looked at him in startled surprise. He cocked an eyebrow at her reaction.

"Did you think everyone is as happy as Yuusuf and Jenna?"

"I guess I do."

"You are naive. It was an arranged marriage that never should have been."

"I've never known anyone as strong as you. Somehow I can't see you meekly doing anyone's bidding—especially in something as important and lasting as marriage," Laura said.

"It is common in our country. On the surface, Yasmine and I were suited. Only the reality proved different."

Laura thought it sounded horrid. For a moment she felt a wave of empathy for the bleak picture his words made.

Unsure what to say, Laura looked beyond him to see Yuusuf and Jenna returning. They were laughing, happy, enjoying each other. How could Tal have agreed to a marriage where he and his wife only *suited* each other. For a moment she felt almost sorry for him.

She saw the moment Yuusuf realized who was seated next to her, noted their pace increased.

"To the rescue," she murmured.

He looked where she looked. "Damn. I think our idyllic time is ending."

"Idyllic?"

"You didn't leave, didn't slap me. We had a conversation for more than ten minutes. It seemed promising. I'll pick you up tomorrow at ten."

"Are you leaving?" she asked.

"Not willingly, but I suspect Yuusuf will have something to say about that," Tal said, rising.

"Tal, we didn't expect to see you here," Yuusuf said when they reached the chaises.

"Your mother told me where to find you. I kept Laura company until you returned."

"I'm sure she appreciates that," Yuusuf said sarcastically.

"Actually, we ended up making a date for tomorrow," Tal said. "One of the cruise ships will be in port tomorrow, and I'm showing it to Laura. Would you and Jenna care to join us?"

"We have plans for tomorrow," Yuusuf said. "As you might already know if you talked with my mother."

"Showing a guest in our country some of our sights is not a crime," Tal said. He pulled his shirt over his head and shucked his shorts. The brief bathing suit hugged every contour. Laura was glad she put on her sunglasses so no one could know how her gaze roved over him. He was magnificent. Muscular where it looked best on men. Not a spare ounce of fat anywhere. The deep tan that covered him gave testament to his hours in the sun. Did he spend every Wednesday afternoon at the beach?

"Come swimming with me," he said to Laura.

"I've been swimming." She might risk seeing him tomorrow, after she had time to prepare her defenses, but she wasn't sure about plunging into the water together this instant. What if he kissed her, held her against that golden body? Her breath caught and she could feel her heart race. Despite everything, hadn't she learned a lesson?

"Maybe another time." He waded out into the water several yards before diving beneath the surface.

"Are you all right?" Jenna asked.

"Actually, I'm fine. Maybe my feelings weren't as engaged as I thought," Laura lied to her friend. She didn't want Jenna to worry about her. She knew the score now, and had no intention of falling more in love with a man who could believe what he had about her. But a few more hours in his company—how could she resist?

Jenna didn't really need her. And the sooner Laura got back to her normal life, the sooner she could put Tal behind her. But until then, would it hurt to spend a little more time together? To be forewarned was to be forearmed.

Laura and the others left before Tal came out of the water. She had longed to linger but dare not confess that to her friends. The hurt still had the power to bring her to her knees. But there was the curiosity, that yearning that wouldn't let her ignore him, much as she thought it might be the wiser course. What she'd learned today gave her new insights into the man.

She wanted him to know beyond a shadow of a doubt she was not the kind of woman who would entice a man for monetary gain. If she gave her heart, it was for love.

Not that she could admit that. She locked that secret away. Maybe years down the road, she'd bring the memories out and reminisce with nostalgia how very special she'd felt for a few days For now, she would make sure the world believed the feelings for Tal had been infatuation—cured by his betrayal.

She just hoped the old adage out of sight out of mind would work a miracle. If so, she'd book her flight home tomorrow.

The next morning Laura awoke with a feeling of anticipation at the prospect of seeing Tal again. Their outing came closer to an armed truce than a date. But she didn't care. She would not confuse the reason for his invitation. He was being politely attentive to someone he'd wronged. As penance, perhaps? She didn't like that idea at all. She wanted him to admit he'd been more than wrong about her.

That was her goal, and she'd work to make him eat crow. Then she'd blithely walk away, honors even.

She arrived at the dining room early for breakfast, only her hostess was present. After breakfast, they walked in the gardens for a short while. Laura told Yvette about the proposed visit to the ship.

"You will wish to sail on one. I've gone several times. It's always such an enjoyable way to travel. Not like planes that leave a body all confused as to the time. I had thought, however, that you and Tal were at odds."

"I think we have a truce in play. For Yuusuf's and Jenna's sakes."

"How civilized of you both," Yvette said. Her eyes twinkled and she smiled at Laura. "I shall look forward to seeing how far the truce goes and how it holds. My nephew is an impatient man, you know."

"I have not seen signs of that," Laura replied. She rather thought Tal very patient, moving deliberately and carefully.

"Time will tell. Run in and get ready. I'll have a maid come get you when he arrives."

The young maid who came to her room later didn't speak English, but Laura had been expecting her and quickly followed her down the corridor to the front foyer. Tal stood near the door, talking with Yvette. He looked up when Laura entered. He was not smiling. She didn't expect the friendly greeting he'd always given in San Francisco. Today he was almost frowning. She glanced at Yvette. Had she said something to anger Tal?

"Ready?" he asked. He looked formidable.

"Yes." For a moment she almost changed her mind. It might be the only time she was able to see a luxury liner. She didn't want to miss her chance.

The sports car was waiting in front of the house. Black and sleek, it looked fast even parked. He held the door for her and she slid onto tanned leather seats. Tal got behind the wheel and soon they were on the main street that led to the heart of the capital. Traffic was heavy. The skyline of the city gleamed in the sun. Sounds and sights and smells swirled around with the windows down and no roof over her head. Laura donned her dark glasses, looking everywhere, enjoying the sensation of wind in her hair, and Tal beside her. For a moment she could only imagine—

Do not go there, she admonished herself. She was merely an obligation for him to discharge. Show her the ship, show Jenna and Yuusuf they could be civilized, return her to Yvette's. End of outing.

As they drew near the docks, Laura began to smell the scent of salt and diesel in the air. She watched as traffic changed from primarily automobiles and buses to large trucks and cargo vans, all headed toward the wharfs.

"Not only cruise ships dock here, I take it," she said, seeing some of the large container vessels like the ones she often saw on San Francisco Bay.

"We have a large shipping industry. The cruise dock is at one end. The rest of the wharf area is for cargo ships, containers and oil," Tal said, winding his way through the traffic effortlessly.

The gleaming white ship that was docked at the last pier stood many stories above street level. Tal parked in a reserved spot and escorted Laura to the wide doors opened on the side of the ship.

"No gangway?" she murmured, a bit disappointed. She'd expected to climb a steep ramp to the main deck.

"Not these days. The door opens at dock level. There are elevators immediately inside to take us wherever we wish. We look to the comfort and convenience of our guests," he said.

They stepped into an elevator on their left and soon arrived at the bridge.

"We'll start our tour here," Tal said.

Laura nodded, looking around with interest. He had not said one word to her beyond what was necessary. The car ride had been virtually silent.

A young, uniformed officer on the bridge studied the charts. He looked up, as if to remind the people the bridge was off-limits. He recognized Tal and almost came to attention. Speaking to him in Arabic, he apparently asked a question, then brushed off an immaculate uniform jacket and nodded politely to Laura.

Tal spoke again, then gestured to Laura. In English he said, "This is the first officer of the ship. He can tell you about the bridge and the responsibilities."

The young man switched to English and began to explain the various duties of the bridge officers controlling the ship when at sea.

The tour continued in a like vein, with Tal finding someone at each point to give Laura a brief explanation of the duties of that station. He'd remain nearby, saying nothing.

"The main dining room," he said two hours later.

Laura had seen the bridge, the luxury state rooms, the lido deck, the main deck, the theater, casinos, spa and gym. She'd heard about tonnage, and passengers complement and the crew. Her head was spinning with facts and figures. She'd learned more than she ever expected, but the day seemed incomplete with Tal ignoring her.

She had planned to ignore him, why did the reverse hurt? How dare he go cold on her!

"I've arranged to lunch here. There are many available seats because of the tours the passengers are taking while in port. Only a few remained on the ship," he said as he showed her to the main dining room.

Lunch was excellent. Their table by the window overlooked the seaside of the harbor and Laura was fascinated by the ships moving in and out. Tal said little, watching the others in the vast dining room.

Piqued, Laura wanted his attention.

"Thank you for inviting me."

"My pleasure," he replied stiffly.

Any foolish hope she might have had that he wanted to see her for herself died. She kicked herself for letting herself get sucked in again. He honored his obligations, even a foolishly made one to someone he didn't particularly like.

Lunch seemed endless because she was so conscious of the man across from her. Gone was the easy camaraderie they'd enjoyed in San Francisco. She felt awkward and out of place. He seemed a million miles away. She wished she had not come.

Once she finished eating, she declined dessert, hoping they'd leave immediately.

"Would you care to see the rest of the ship?" he asked.

"I've seen more than I ever expected. I'd rather return to the villa."

"As you wish."

They drove back in silence. Laura wished she could find something to say that would ease the tension, but words wouldn't come.

When he pulled up in front of Yvette's villa, Laura didn't wait for him to open her door, but quickly got out on her own.

"Thanks for the tour," she said, preparing to dash into the house.

"Wait, Laura." He got out of the car, leaning on the door and looking at her.

"I have a favor to ask you," Tal said.

She blinked. He wanted to ask her a favor? Had that been the reason for the tour of the ship?

"And that is?" she said cautiously.

He came around the car, holding her gaze. When he was only two feet away, he stopped.

"My cousin and his fiancée are being honored at a party given by his aunt Sarah on Friday."

She nodded. She knew that.

"Yvette suggested it be better if I not attend."

Laura watched him warily. If they didn't want him, what was that to her? For a moment she breathed easier. She wouldn't have to maintain her happy facade.

"Yuusuf is my cousin. He and I used to be close. I care for him a great deal. I fear my not being present would give rise to gossip that would hurt the family."

"Did you tell them that?" she asked.

"I told Yvette. She said Jenna was looking out for her friend—you. I know I have no right to ask, but if you would grant me this favor, I would appreciate it."

"What favor?"

"Tell Jenna that you wouldn't mind if I came to the party."

Laura stared at him. "Why would I do that? I would mind. I don't care if I never see you again."

"After today? I thought you enjoyed seeing the ship."

"Was that what this was all about? Not fulfilling an obligation from an earlier time, but to placate me, butter me up so I'd agree to tell Jenna to invite you? It won't work. I'm humiliated that you have used me. I thought you were wonderful. So handsome and so attentive. I've never had such attention paid to me as you did. It was glorious. And it was as false as a three-dollar bill. Do you know how humiliating it is to have people hold such an awful opinion of me and treat me with such disdain? I wouldn't treat anyone the way you treated me. Jenna knows that. I can't just say, oh well, it was no big deal. She'd never believe me."

Laura turned and went to the front door, opening it, thankful no one felt the need to lock it.

Quietly she shut it and went directly to her room. Grateful she met no one in the passage way, Laura was almost shaking with emotions. She hated the position Tal had put her in. Hated the fact he'd never been serious about her for an instant when she'd thought she'd met the man she could love all her life.

She hated the fact she'd fallen in love with the man. How dumb did that make her? She'd actually trusted him when all of the evidence suggested otherwise.

Kicking off her shoes, she flopped back on the bed, staring up at the ceiling. Burned into her mind was his face as she'd last seen it, bleak and hard. He'd not asked the favor lightly, she knew. He was a proud man, and asking her to grant him clemency must have been hard to do.

"Serves him right," she muttered. She hoped he regretted every moment he'd lied to her. That he was an outcast to his family for the rest of his life.

She rolled over.

No, she did not wish that on him. She knew how important family was. She'd been cherished by her grandparents after her parents' death. Now they, too, were gone. She didn't have a cousin ready to step in and do anything to save her if he thought she were making a mistake. She didn't have her grandparents, who would have moved mountains to make sure she was happy.

Were Tal and his grandfather so different from her own family? Wouldn't her own grandfather have done whatever he felt needed doing to keep his girl happy and safe? No matter what the cost to a stranger?

Tal had acted for the good of his family. It was unfortunate she'd been the collateral damage. He hadn't known her, only feared Yuusuf was repeating a mistake he'd obviously made more than once. He'd gone at the request of his grandfather.

Had her grandfather asked her to do something, she would have gladly complied. She'd loved him.

Tears seeped from her eyes. That was the whole crux of the matter. Tal loved Yuusuf, their grandfather loved them both, Yuusuf loved Jenna. It was only Laura who was left out in the cold and that hurt.

But keeping Tal from his family was wrong, no

matter how much satisfaction she might think she'd derive. What if something happened to one of them, as the unthinkable had happened with her own parents dying too young?

Laura spent an hour arguing with herself, but finally common decency prevailed. She washed her face and brushed her hair. Donning her shoes, she went to find Jenna.

CHAPTER TEN

TAL was hard at work that afternoon when Yuusuf
called.

"Your plan obviously worked," Yuusuf said.

"What plan?"

"To get Laura to change her mind about you. Did
she fall in love with ship, or did you promise her something in exchange for telling Jenna she was no longer
mad at you?"

For a moment Tal was confused. Laura had told
Jenna that? After her scathing denouncement in front
of Yvette's house? What had changed in the interven-
ing three hours?

"Anyway, the family will be gathering at Sophia's
early to have a light supper before the engagement party.
We would like you to be there at six, if you will come."

Tal had heard more gracious invitations in his life.
But he didn't quibble. His curiosity was growing. What
had Laura told Jenna, and why?

"I shall be happy to attend."

"Just stay away from Laura."

"Is that a condition she made?"

"No, it's one I'm making. If I can get through this visit with Jenna happy, I'll be content. I don't want you messing with her friend and upsetting her again. They're closer than sisters."

Tal was again surprised at his cousin's stance. He and his grandfather had been wrong. Yuusuf had grown up.

"I do not plan to upset her."

Yuusuf took a breath Tal could hear across the telephone wires. "I hope you two can maintain a truce. I wanted you for my best man. We are marrying in San Francisco, and of course Jenna will have Laura as her maid of honor."

"You make up your own mind, Yuusuf. I did what I felt was needed. If you can't accept that, and my apology, then say so. What is done is done. I hope Laura will forgive the deception one day."

"I'm not sure she ever will, or Jenna. She was falling in love with you, Tal. Couldn't you see that?"

"With me or the money I represented?" he couldn't help asking.

"She is not Yasmine. I knew more than you suspected about the hellish marriage you had. But Laura is nothing like that."

"All women are, to one degree or another," Tal said.

"Not Laura. At least not according to Jenna. You know how much money her parents have. Laura and Jenna are so close you'd think nothing of Laura accepting gifts from her best friend. It was an argument they'd had as teenagers, and it's stuck ever since. Laura is her friend, but refuses to accept anything from Jenna in a material way. Even their birthday presents and Christmas gifts have a twenty-dollar limit. They enjoy seeing what unusual items they can get each other for so little. I don't believe Laura was after your money any more than Jenna was after mine."

Tal had seen in Laura a woman greedy for trinkets, who had hinted about a cruise ship as if blatantly indicating she'd be happy with a free cruise. But that was what he'd been looking for. Had any of it been real?

"Tell me about Laura," he said, throwing down his pen and leaning back in the high desk chair.

"You dated her for two weeks, what's there for me to tell? I don't know her all that well myself. It's Jenna I had fallen in love with, not Laura. We saw her from time to time, of course, and Jenna talks about her as if she is a sister. She was really happy Laura had found someone special. Apparently she'd never fallen in love before. She's dated, but never found the right man. Guess she didn't this time, either."

Tal winced. Yuusuf was right. He had not been the right man for Laura.

"Anyway, whatever you said to her today worked. She's convinced Jenna that she would be fine with you being at all family gatherings. She's returning home on Saturday."

When Tal hung up a few moments later, all urge for work had disappeared. He remembered his father saying one time he would never understand women when his mother had done something that had baffled him. Tal knew exactly how he felt. The last thing he expected was for Laura to convince Jenna she was no longer upset. Especially after their parting.

* * *

Laura bid her hostess good-night early. She was tired and wanted to get a good night's sleep. Today had been hectic. With the party preparations underway, she offered to help any way she could. There wasn't much to be done except for Laura and Jenna to go shopping for new dresses. And have their hair done on Friday afternoon.

Laura tried to be enthusiastic. She was marking time, trying to appear carefree and happy for her friend. But as the hours slowly passed, all she could think of was soon she'd be on a plane for home and all artificiality could end.

It had taken quite a bit of convincing for Jenna to believe that Laura would be all right with Tal being at the party. It was only at dinner that Laura heard Tal was going to be Yuusuf's best man. She should have expected it. But it still came as a shock. By the time the wedding came round, she'd be over the man. Maybe even be able to laugh about her infatuation.

Lying in bed an hour later, Laura couldn't sleep. She finally gave up tossing and turning and rose pulling on the light robe that covered her summer nightie. The warm night air beckoned. A walk in the garden would be perfect. She'd enjoy the quiet and get some fresh air which might help her sleep.

Just as she was about to step outside, she saw a shadow. A second later there was a light tap at the window. "Laura?"

"Tal?" She stepped out onto the patio by the doors. He turned and stepped closer.

"You were awake?"

"I was coming out for a walk. What are you doing here?" Their voices were low.

"I came to talk to you. When I arrived, Yvette said you'd already gone to bed. She then spent the next several moments telling me everything Yuusuf and Jenna have done since they arrived. She would make an excellent reporter."

"She's happy her son has found his soul mate, I think."

"Soul mate, do you think?" he asked softly. "Come, walk with me. The moon is bright."

"I was planning to take a walk, though I'm hardly dressed to be seen by anyone. I thought I'd be alone."

"It's dark, no one will see us."

"I meant you," she grumbled, but stepped away from the shadows of the house to follow the path leading to the fountain. Would it be running this late? A moment later she knew it was, she could hear the splash of water, almost feel the coolness as they reached the benches nearby.

"Why are you here, Tal?" she asked, sitting on the bench still warm from the sun. He sat beside her, near enough she felt the heat from his thigh. She swallowed hard, feeling that fluttering that came whenever he was close.

"I came to thank you for changing Jenna's mind about my attending their party." He took her hand. "I appreciate that. Family is important to me."

Laura went still. She could scarcely breathe. Pulling her hand free, she crossed her arms, removing temptation from Tal's path.

"Family is important to everyone, or it should be."

* * *

Tal wanted to sweep her into his arms, to promise her she would never be alone again. That there would always be family enough for her. The unexpected emotion caught him by surprise. She was a woman, not some little girl. She didn't need him or his family.

And that truth hurt.

"It there a way to start over?" he asked softly. He'd been wrong. He hated that. But more importantly, he knew he'd destroyed something precious. Something fragile and not easily replaced.

She shook her head. "I don't see one. I'll be leaving on Saturday. We can stay out of each other's way until then."

His hand brushed back the hair from her cheek, the breeze kept tendrils floating around her face. Her skin was so soft. He wished he could see her better. The moon gave enough light to walk the path, but didn't come beneath the trellis where they sat.

"I will miss the woman who loved the hot-air balloon ride," he said gently.

He'd been completely wrong about her. He wanted to go back, reestablish trust between them, but didn't know how. She wasn't helping. Was there more to their relationship than he had suspected? Yuusuf mentioned love. Was it at all possible?

One way to find out.

He drew her into his arms. For a moment she resisted, then seemed to melt into his embrace. This was what he'd been missing since their night at Lake Tahoe. She felt feminine and sweet. Yet she fired a hunger in him he'd never known before. Each moment with her was special, and he, like a fool, had thrown it all away.

Or maybe not. She returned his kiss as if she meant it. Then she pushed him away.

"That's not solving anything," she said, jumping up and running down the path.

Tal knew it solved nothing, but it gave him an entirely new aspect to consider.

He rose.

Laura reached her room out of breath. How could she be such an idiot to kiss the man! Good heavens, hadn't she learned anything? Her heart raced. Her mouth was warm from his. Licking her lips, she could still taste the kiss. Her skin felt too tight.

"Laura." Tal strode into the room from the garden.

"You can't come in here." She turned to face him. "What if Yvette or someone hears you?"

"I'm not staying, though I wouldn't mind. I want new terms."

"Terms, for what?"

"For what we have between us. A truce maybe?"

"There is nothing between us, you made sure of that."

"That's what I want to change."

"What are you talking about?"

"About getting to know each other—the real person we both are, not some preconceived notion of who each other is."

"I had no preconceived idea. I thought you were from England, an ordinary man who was interested in me."

"I am."

"No."

He reached out and clasped her shoulders, drawing her closer. "I've apologized until I'm blue in the face. I'm done. I'm sorry for the way I treated you, but not that we met. I want you, Laura, any way I can get you."

"Are you crazy?"

His kiss stopped her thought process. He molded her body to his, encircling her with his arms, holding her close, as if cherished. His kiss deepened, took Laura to heights she'd never gone before. She would hate herself later, was the last thought she had, before giving herself to his embrace. She loved this man. This may be the last time they'd ever be alone together. Why not take advantage of what he so generously offered?

Time had no meaning. She wasn't sure if she was still in Tamarin or floating into the nighttime sky. Tal filled her senses, brought exquisite sensations never before dreamed of. Her heart engaged, her mind free. Nothing had made sense since the day she'd returned from Lake Tahoe and discovered the truth.

But what was the truth? That she loved him? That he was trying to cement a friendship to keep his cousin happy? Could she fault him for that?

A sound in the hallway had them pull back. For a moment both of them seemed to hold their breath. Nothing further.

"I have to go," he said, kissing her gently, nibbling slightly against her lips. "I don't want to."

She pulled back. "But you must."

"I know." Another kiss. "Will you think about what I've said?"

"I might." How could she think about anything else?

"Come to dinner with me tomorrow night."

She was tempted. "I don't know."

"I'll call you in the morning." Another kiss and he was gone.

Laura went to the French doors and looked out, but she couldn't see or hear him. Had it all been a dream?

The way her body hummed, it had been very real.

Sleep was a long time in coming. But she was not going for another walk in the gardens.

What did Tal really want from her?

"You are certifiably crazy, you know that?" Jenna said the next evening, lounging on Laura's bed, watching her friend dress.

"Probably. I thought you'd be glad to see I'm not holding a grudge."

"You're putting yourself in harm's way," Jenna said.

"Hardly that."

"To the safety of your heart," she muttered.

Laura turned and looked at her friend. "Jenna, this is just dinner. I want you to know Tal and I can be cordial to each other. Your wedding is important to me. I wouldn't have it jeopardized in any way. Besides, I am looking forward to seeing more of Tamarin."

"So Yuusuf and I will take you around."

"No, this is a special time for the two of you. Spend it together."

Jenna didn't argue with that, but from the frown on her face, she still wasn't pleased with Laura's idea of cementing a détente with Yuusuf's cousin.

"If he doesn't treat you right, I'll know."

Laura laughed. It was that or give into the bleakness she held tightly hidden. She expected Tal to be charming, turning the knife of what could have been if things had been different. This time, she was going on a date with her eyes wide-open and no expectations. She hoped they'd enjoy the evening. But she had no daydreams of forever.

"How do you like the dress?" she asked, hoping to change the subject. She and Jenna and Yvette had gone shopping earlier. She had to admire the Frenchwoman's idea of style. The dress made her look exotic and sophisticated. It was of gold, with a bias cut that displayed every bit of her figure to advantage.

"On you it looks wonderful. Makes your eyes seem smoky or something, and gives your skin a glow. I hope Tal falls in love with you so you can knock him over and walk away victorious."

Laura laughed. "Jenna, this isn't warfare."

"Isn't it? Why all the ammunition?"

Laura glanced back into the mirror. She did look like she was out to capture hearts, or at least the fascinated interest of one particular man. "Maybe just a tiny skirmish, I'd like him to regret our never becoming a couple," she admitted honestly.

"You do still have feelings for him," Jenna said triumphantly.

"Whether I do or not, I'm keeping them to myself." Laura took one last look and prepared to leave. Tal would arrive soon to pick her up.

She, Yvette and Jenna were in the formal salon when

he arrived. He came in to greet the others. "Ready?" he asked Laura, his gaze traveling down the length of her.

She knew by the gleam in his eye he approved of how she looked.

"Don't make a late night of it," Yvette warned, her eyes watching Tal. "Tomorrow's the engagement party and Laura will need to get a lot of sleep so she can stay up to the end."

Tonight Tal had the top off the sports car. He ushered Laura in, and soon they were on their way.

"Where are we going?" she asked.

"You'll see," was all he said. He turned on the radio and tuned it into a station playing soft music. Again the ride was silent, except for the music. She couldn't help compare it to the ride to Lake Tahoe, when they'd talked and talked.

Tamarin was not built on hills like San Francisco. It was primarily flat, at sea level, only in the distance did the horizon rise toward the Atlas mountains of North Africa. The modern buildings vied with each other to stand as the dominant feature on the landscape. The wide expanse of glass walls reflected each other and the setting sun. It looked as if they were painted with the sunset.

It was still light and she could see all the way to the Mediterranean Sea. Large ships sailed near the horizon. Was one of them the cruise ship she'd toured a couple of days ago?

The cityscape gave way to residential, which soon seemed to melt into the countryside.

"Where are we going?" she asked again.

"Here," he said, turning into a long driveway, flanked by tall flowering oleander. They rode to a house sitting in darkness, the scent of the sea filled the air. He stopped to the side of the villa and turned off the engine. It was quiet, only the cooling of the engine and the sound of crickets could be heard. And the soft murmur of the sea.

"And this is where?" Laura asked, looking around. The gardens were more formal than Yvette's. The house was terra cotta in color, with deep olive-green trim.

"This is my home. I have had the cook prepare our meal to be eaten on the patio behind the house."

He helped her from the car, but when he reached to take her hand, Laura pulled it away. She walked around the house on the wide path, and stopped when she saw the beautiful setup on the patio.

Candles in lanterns encircled the wide patio. They were scarcely noticeable in the still light sky, but later, when night fell, they would lend a magical feel to the setting.

A small table had been set near the edge closest to the sea, candles glimmering on it as well. She stepped closer, enjoying the sea breeze caressing her skin.

"It's enchanting."

"Come, as soon as we are seated, the servants will begin to serve the meal."

As if watching from a window, as soon as they were at the table, a man in a snowy-white jacket brought out beverages and an antipasto tray.

"I ordered a typical Tasmainian dish. It's a kind of stew, savory and delicious, I think you will enjoy it."

Tal could tell Laura remained wary. He did not want that. His hope was to soothe her with fine food, show her his home and ease back into the friendship they had shared in California. He acknowledged that it would be difficult. But not impossible. She could not have responded to his kisses as she had were she indifferent.

"Is this the home you shared with your wife?" she asked.

"Yes. I brought Yasmine here after we married. I inherited this property from my mother's father. I was the oldest grandson in that family. My grandmother died before he did, so he left it to me."

"You were fortunate."

The daylight was waning. The moon was still almost full, riding low on the horizon. Soon it would bathe everything in an ephemeral light. After dinner he'd take Laura for a walk along his private beach. They could dance at the water's edge if they chose.

By the time the main course was served, the natural light had faded. The candles illuminated the patio. Tal studied Laura while she ate, looking away when she raised her eyes to his. He'd never seen a more lovely woman.

"You aren't eating," she said.

"I was waiting for it to cool." He took a bite. "Tell me all about Laura Toliver."

"You've heard my story before," she said.

"I haven't heard where you went to school and what kind of little girl you were. Nor what are your dreams and hopes for the future."

She was silent for a moment and he suspected he knew what she was thinking—he could have had all that and more, once.

"I was a good little girl, loved by her parents until

they died, and then by my grandparents. I have some friends, like Jenna, whom I've known all my life. Some newer ones I've met since college and at work. My hopes are to be happy in the future."

"Are you not happy now?"

She hesitated so long he thought she wasn't going to respond.

"Tonight, right this moment, I'm…content."

He hoped for more.

She smiled at him sadly. "I almost did a background check on you. I called your friend Earl, but he had left for Japan. You should tell him not to announce that on his answering machine, what if someone called casing the place?"

"I'll make a note to tell him. Why did you want to do a trace? Do I look like a crook to you?"

"No, but not telling us your last name was a red flag, or very romantic. I chose to see it one way. Jason the other."

"Smith is hard to trace."

"I knew that wasn't your last name. You wanted us to know you were not giving out that information."

"So I can thank Earl for not blowing my cover by taking his trip to Japan."

"Actually, I decided it would show a definite lack of trust if I did something like that," she said.

That stung. She had trusted him. And he had let her down.

"You can trust me, Laura," he said. "We have no more secrets."

"No need. We mean nothing to each other. You were right, this is delicious."

Tal was annoyed by the way she kept turning away from the possibility of their seeing each other. "I'm pleased you like it. Want to hear about when I was a boy?"

"If you wish to tell me."

Her indifference was frustrating.

"I went to school here until I was twelve, then to boarding school in England."

"The reason for your charming accent."

"At least you find something charming about me," he bit out.

"Oh, Tal, when you try, you are charm personified."

"You make it sound false."

"Wasn't it?"

He drew a deep breath. For someone who said she wanted to call a truce, she seemed to be deliberately goading him.

Tal began a long story about his university studies, and his early forays into the business world, culminating with his father turning over the reins of the cruise line only three years ago. Tal's assessment was his father saw it as a way to move on without Yasmine.

Laura seemed to be listening attentively, but Tal felt he couldn't be sure.

When the plates were cleared, Tal told his servant to hold dessert, he and his guest would walk along the beach first. The man bowed and continued to remove the dishes.

"If you are finished, I thought we could walk along the shore," he said to Laura in English.

She placed her napkin on the table and rose. "If you don't mind, I'd rather return home. I mean, to Yvette's. She's right, it'll be a long evening tomorrow night."

"Running away?" he said, in hopes of goading her.

"Strategic retreat," she retorted, standing tall.

"Sounds like advance and parry, to me," he said.

"What?"

"Fencing terms. I advance, you push me aside. Only you don't seem to advance."

"What is it you want, Tal?"

"I told you, I want you."

"For how long?"

Tal stared at her. He didn't have a timetable. However long they enjoyed each other's company, he supposed. He knew he didn't want her to fly home Saturday and he not see her again until Yuusuf's wedding.

"Never mind," she said before he could rely. "It doesn't matter. You would forever wonder if I was after your wealth and I would forever wonder if you thought I was."

"No."

"Please, just take me back."

Laura watched the other cars on the road as they drove. It seemed they were destined to travel without speaking. She could feel the anger shimmering off Tal, but she didn't care. She was tired, a bit depressed, and anxious to get the next day finished so she could go home.

CHAPTER ELEVEN

YVETTE insisted they all take early naps and once refreshed, they had appointments to have their hair and nails done. Laura loved being pampered at the salon Yvette frequented. She had her nails done with French tips, and her toes in a color to match the red dress she was wearing that evening. The day at the beach had given her skin a healthy glow, and she knew she'd look her best for her friend's engagement party and formal announcement.

Jenna's parents had flown in last night and were staying at a hotel in the downtown area. Yvette had invited them to stay with her, but they preferred the hotel. Yuusuf was seeing that they reached his aunt Sophia's home early for the family dinner. It would be the first time they met Yuusuf's family.

"I could get used to this," Jenna said, leaning back as her feet were massaged prior to having her toenails painted.

"You probably will," Laura said lazily.

"Nope, I still have my work at home. Yuusuf has agreed it's important."

Laura was happy her friend would still live nearby. She drifted almost to sleep as Yvette and Jenna made plans for Yuusuf's mother to come to San Francisco to visit soon.

Not for the first time, Laura thought as she drifted along, she wished she were planning a wedding of her own.

Sophia's house was a two-story home she and her physician husband owned in another part of the city from where Yvette lived. The homes seemed more western in style. There were parking attendants to take cars as people arrived, driving them elsewhere to keep the flow moving. With the family arriving early, they had little to do as yet.

Sophia greeted Laura almost as warmly as she did Jenna. She directed everyone to a small dining room where a buffet supper had been set up. While not as formal as dinner at Yvette's Laura still had butterflies. Especially when she saw Tal. He nodded a greeting from across the room, but made no effort to speak to her.

During the meal, she sat beside Jenna's mother on one side and another cousin of Yuusuf's on the other, Nura. Her command of English was not as fluent as her male cousins. Still, Laura found they had a common ground when speaking about their love of paintings.

All too soon it was time to greet the arriving guests.

Laura entered the large ballroom where friends and relatives gathered. It began to slowly fill with men and women in evening clothes that were as colorful as they were expensive. Bemused by the ease in which everyone was able to communicate, Laura wished she could speak a second language. She felt very isolated by her lack of Arabic. Many of the people present seemed to speak some English.

Once or twice she caught a glimpse of Tal. He was always surrounded by several people and seemed to be quite popular with a number of young women.

She looked around, feeling left out. Watching other people was part of her job, but she was a guest at this event. Still, it was like she'd thought it would be the time she and Tal had discussed his taking her to a party like this. Her world was too removed from the others to belong.

As soon as the last guest had arrived, the orchestra began to play and Jenna and Yuusuf moved onto the clear area of the room to begin to dance.

After a circuit, others joined them.

"May I have this dance?" Tal said, holding out his hand.

Laura put hers in his without thinking.

They moved in time to the music, she with her eyes closed, savoring every bittersweet moment.

"Are you enjoying the party?" he asked softly in her ear.

"I feel like I should be noting suspicious-looking people in case they are casing the place for a heist," she replied, opening her eyes.

He was gazing down at her, his face close to hers.

"You're not working tonight. Enjoy yourself."

"Yes." Now I am.

"Have you met everyone?"

She laughed. "Are you kidding? There are more than a hundred people here. I sat next to Nura at dinner. She was delightful. And I know some of Yuusuf's family. I saw your grandparents, Yvette's parents. No one wants to meet me. I'm not the guest of honor."

"You underestimate yourself. There are a number of people who wish to meet you."

As if he conjured one up, a man tapped him on the shoulder. "May I?" he asked.

Tal scowled but relinquished Laura.

"Good evening," the man said, beginning to dance with her. "I am Mohammed, Nura's brother. She told me she enjoyed discussing art at dinner."

"We did. How nice to meet you." She gave a bright smile and set out to enjoy the evening.

About eleven-thirty, Laura was ready to return to Yvette's place and go to bed. Her feet hurt. Her cheeks hurt from smiling so much and she was getting confused with all the names of the people she'd met. After Mohammed, there had been several other young men who wanted to dance. She'd met some friends of Yuusuf and Jenna with whom she was able to have a lively conversation.

She kept an eye out for Tal, but he seemed to have disappeared.

The formal announcement of the engagement between Yuusuf and Jenna was to be made at midnight. The celebration party was all Jenna could have hoped for. But midnight was still some time away and she was tired.

She found Jenna. "Think I can ask Yvette for a ride back as soon as the announcement is made?"

"Oh, don't leave. You can't," Jenna said.

"This is your night. It's late and my feet hurt. You and

Yuusuf enjoy every minute. But I want to go back as soon as I hear the announcement."

Jenna bit her lip. "Wait just a bit. I know, go to the library. You can sit down for a while, but make sure you get back here before midnight."

Laura went down the hall to the closed door of the library. Slipping inside, she breathed a sigh of relief at the silence. It was refreshing after the noise of the crowd. She'd sit for a couple of minutes, return to the ballroom for the announcement and then slip away.

The room had only one lamp on, near a chair by the window. She walked farther into the room, startled to see Tal rise.

"Tal?" She looked around. He was alone. "What are you doing here?"

"I came to escape."

"Me, too." She crossed to the matching chair and sat down. Easing her feet from her shoes, she wiggled her toes and leaned her head back. "I'm tired."

"It's late. May I take you home?"

She looked at him. "I'm sure I can get a ride after the announcement. I want to be here for that. I didn't see you for a good part of the evening." She closed her eyes. She didn't need to tell him that.

"I had some things to attend to."

"Work? On the night of Yuusuf's engagement party?"

"Some things can't wait." He reached into his pocket and pulled out a golden bracelet. The charms dangled from the links, their jewels sparkling in the lamplight.

"I want you to have this, Laura. To remember the

happy times we shared. You can't deny you enjoyed yourself. Think about the day of our balloon ride. How soaring over the valley was so special. The picnic lunch we shared. Or the walk along Lake Tahoe we took before going home that Sunday. Maybe you won't wear it soon, but one day?"

She looked at it with longing. She had enjoyed every moment with him—until she'd found out the truth. In later years it would be the only tangible thing she had from Tal. She knew he would never give it to anyone else.

Slowly she extended her arm. He fastened it around her wrist, then kissed her hand.

She noticed a fourth charm—of Lake Tahoe. "Thank you." Resignedly she admitted the jewels on all the charms were likely the real thing. But it wasn't for its monetary value she'd cherish it.

"My pleasure. At the risk of getting you angry again, I'll admit to another deception. I asked Jenna to get you to come here."

"Why?"

"I wanted to ask you to stay?"

"Beyond tomorrow?"

"Yes, beyond tomorrow."

She sat up, fumbling for her shoes. "I can't do that."

"I want you to marry me, Laura," he said in a low voice.

Stunned, she looked at him. "No."

"No?"

"I can't marry you."

"Yuusuf was wrong then."

"What does he have to do with anything?"

"He suggested you might be in love with me."

She would give him a piece of her mind when she saw him again.

"The man is crazy." She stood. He rose as well.

"I had an interesting conversation today with Jenna's father. And he made a suggestion I thought was well said."

"What?" she asked.

He withdrew an envelope from his jacket pocket and handed it to her.

"What is this?"

"It's several hundred shares of my cruise ship line."

"What? I can't take that." She pushed the envelope back toward him, but Tal stepped back, his hands going behind his back.

"According to Jenna's father, you have almost a phobia about people thinking you are using them. Apparently your grandparents instilled that in you—never take anything from anyone. Even someone who loves you as Jenna does. Pride is a wonderful thing, unless it becomes too inflexible."

"I'm not taking this from you," she said, tossing the envelope on the chair he'd vacated.

"I spend a lot of time taking care of the transactions. The shares are yours whether you walk out with them in hand or not."

"Why?" She didn't understand at all. She'd told him she wasn't after anything. She'd done nothing to make him think she wanted his money.

"I want you to be wealthy."

"What?"

"So when I ask you to marry me you won't ever suspect I think it's because you are after my money."

Laura stared at him. Had she heard him right? "No."

"The shares are yours regardless of your answer. I had hoped it would be yes."

She stormed to the door. "I can't believe you. Take the shares or I'll shred them."

"They will still be registered in your name. Replacement paper will be issued."

"Unregister them."

"I cannot do that."

"Can I?"

He shook his head.

"I bet I can."

"I'll issue more."

Once again the absurdity struck her, only it saddened her this time. She didn't want his charity.

What she wanted was what he wasn't giving.

"No, Tal." She opened the door.

"I love you, Laura."

She stopped, hovering on the brink of delight. Had she heard him right, or had she imagined the words? She shut the door, leaned against it and looked at him. "What?"

He came purposely across the room. "I love you. I want you to marry me, stay here in Tamarin with me, travel with me, have children with me, grow old with me."

"What about your parents?"

"What about them?"

"They didn't pick me."

"No, this time I picked. For once I took a lesson from my younger cousin—to find a woman to love."

He stopped with his toes almost touching hers, his breath fanned across her cheeks. She felt hemmed in. Her heart was almost bursting with joy.

"You really love me? How can I trust you. How can you be sure I don't want your wealth and not you?" Laura could not believe what she was hearing. Where was the catch?

He laughed and caught her in his arms. "Not after this. I never saw anyone so reluctant to take some shares in a profitable business."

"I don't want them, I only want you," she said, just before his kissed her.

The kiss was interrupted by a knock on the door. Jenna poked her head inside. When she saw them, she smiled and pushed into the room. "Yes!" she cried, Yuusuf at her shoulder.

Reaching out to hug Laura, she glanced at Tal. "This better mean what I think it does."

Tal frowned. "You're too soon. I haven't given her the ring yet."

"I haven't said yes," Laura said.

"Go, we'll be there in a minute," Tal instructed.

Jenna laughed and almost danced.

Tal brought out a small box and opened it, showing Jenna. The ring was lovely, not at all ostentatious, but perfect in every regard.

"I'll ask again, will you marry me?" he said, taking her hand and kissing it.

"If you really love me and know and believe and affirm that I love you and only you and not your money or cruise ship line or jewelry you give me—"

He placed his fingers against her lips.

"That I know."

He slipped the ring on her finger and kissed her again.

Hands linked, they returned to the ballroom. Yuusuf, Jenna, her parents and Salilk bin Horah were standing near the dias on which the orchestra sat. Tal led Laura over. His grandfather lifted an eyebrow and Tal raised their linked hand, the diamond glittering.

Taking the microphone, Salilk cleared his throat. Everyone in the room stopped talking.

"In honor of our guests, I am making this announcement first in English. I will repeat in Arabic for our friends who don't speak that language." He repeated the sentence in Arabic.

"I'm an old man. I have lived a good life, and hope to continue to do so. Tonight my heart is happy as I have the pleasure of seeing the beginning to a new generation of my family. Tonight I announce the engagement of my two grandsons, Yuusuf bin Mohammad bin Horah to Miss Jenna Stanhope of the United States and Talique bin Azoz bin Al-Rahman to Miss Laura Toliver of the United States. I wish both couples long lives, happiness and many great-grand-children, as I hope they will provide for me." He repeated the words in Arabic, and a cheer went up from the crowd.

Jenna grinned at her friend. "We thought Tal would never pop the question," she whispered through the din. "Best friends forever?"

"Forever. Right behind Yuusuf and Tal," Laura said,

turning to kiss her future husband amidst the cheering and well wishes of the family that was now to become hers. She knew he truly would be her best friend, lover and husband forever.

If you enjoyed what you just read,
then we've got an offer you can't resist!

Take 2 bestselling love stories FREE!

Plus get a FREE surprise gift!

Clip this page and mail it to Harlequin Reader Service®

IN U.S.A.
3010 Walden Ave.
P.O. Box 1867
Buffalo, N.Y. 14240-1867

IN CANADA
P.O. Box 609
Fort Erie, Ontario
L2A 5X3

YES! Please send me 2 free Harlequin Romance® novels and my free surprise gift. After receiving them, if I don't wish to receive anymore, I can return the shipping statement marked cancel. If I don't cancel, I will receive 6 brand-new novels every month, before they're available in stores! In the U.S.A., bill me at the bargain price of $3.57 plus 25¢ shipping & handling per book and applicable sales tax, if any*. In Canada, bill me at the bargain price of $4.05 plus 25¢ shipping & handling per book and applicable taxes**. That's the complete price and a savings of 10% off the cover prices—what a great deal! I understand that accepting the 2 free books and gift places me under no obligation ever to buy any books. I can always return a shipment and cancel at any time. Even if I never buy another book from Harlequin, the 2 free books and gift are mine to keep forever.

186 HDN DZ72
386 HDN DZ73

Name	(PLEASE PRINT)	
Address	Apt.#	
City	State/Prov.	Zip/Postal Code

Not valid to current Harlequin Romance® subscribers.
Want to try another series? Call 1-800-873-8635
or visit www.morefreebooks.com.

* Terms and prices subject to change without notice. Sales tax applicable in N.Y.
** Canadian residents will be charged applicable provincial taxes and GST.
All orders subject to approval. Offer limited to one per household.
® are registered trademarks owned and used by the trademark owner and or its licensee.

HROM04R   ©2004 Harlequin Enterprises Limited

HOTEL MARCHAND

Four sisters.
A family legacy.
And someone is out to destroy it.

A captivating new limited continuity, launching June 2006

The most beautiful hotel in New Orleans,
and someone is out to destroy it. But mystery,
danger and some surprising family revelations
and discoveries won't stop the Marchand sisters
from protecting their birthright…
and finding love along the way.

SPECIAL PRICE!

HOTEL MARCHAND

This riveting new saga begins with

In the Dark

by national bestselling author

JUDITH ARNOLD

The party at Hotel Marchand is in full swing when the lights suddenly go out. What does head of security Mac Jensen do first? He's torn between two jobs—protecting the guests at the hotel and keeping the woman he loves safe.

A woman to protect. A hotel to secure. And no idea who's determined to harm them.

On Sale June 2006

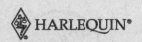
HARLEQUIN®

HARLEQUIN ROMANCE®

Coming Next Month

#3903 A NINE-TO-FIVE AFFAIR Jessica Steele

Emily Lawson is caring for her beloved grandmother, but her gorgeous boss Barden Cunningham doesn't know this—he thinks that she's not taking her work seriously. Things get worse when she drives through snow to deliver a report to Barden and crashes her car. When she's forced to stay with him, Emily realizes that seeing him out of work is quite different from sharing an office!

#3904 HAVING THE FRENCHMAN'S BABY Rebecca Winters

Rachel Valentine is a wine buyer for the Valentine family's exclusive Bella Lucia restaurants and her relationship with winemaker Luc Chartier should be strictly business. Seduced by the vineyards and Luc, Rachel falls in love. But their one night of passion is followed by a shocking revelation about Luc's past. Heartbroken, Rachel returns home to find that she is pregnant.

#3905 SAYING YES TO THE BOSS Jackie Braun

Regina Bellini doesn't believe in love at first sight, but then she is forced to work for the one man who makes her heart stand still—Dane Conlan. The storm brewing within her is undeniable, and that could be enough to tempt her into saying yes to her boss, in spite of what—and who—stands between them.

#3906 WIFE AND MOTHER WANTED Nicola Marsh

Brody Elliott is a single dad struggling to bring up his daughter, Molly. Brody is determined to protect his little girl from heartbreak again. So when Molly befriends their pretty new neighbor, Clarissa Lewis, Brody is wary. Clarissa instantly bonds with Molly. If only Brody was willing to let go of his past and give in to their attraction, maybe Clarissa could be his, too.